CLAIMED BY THE ORC

ORCS UNCHAINED

LESLIE CHASE

Claimed by the Orc
Copyright 2024 Leslie Chase
All rights reserved

This is a work of fiction intended for mature audiences. All names, characters, businesses, places, events and incidents are products of the author's imagination. Any resemblance to actual persons, living or dead, or actual events is purely coincidental.

❦ Created with Vellum

*For Mabl, you know what you did.
And Alana Khan, who's idea this was*

1

GRAGASH

The crowd roared, and for a moment I forgot it all. My pain, my shame, my fears. Everything faded as hundreds of people screamed for me. The bright glare of the arena lights blinded me to the audience, turning them into shadows which crowded around the cage I stepped into, the cage which would be my entire universe until the fight was done.

I breathed deep, drawing in a lungful of cheap beer and expensive blood, the stale smell of sweat, and the harsh smell of ozone. The sawdust covering the floor gave my feet purchase, a pleasant change from the mirror-finish chrome I'd fought on last.

"**Gra**-gash, **Gra**-gash, **Gra**-gash." My fans in the crowd chanted my name, and I turned, fist raised, to roar back at them. As always, the chant skipped a beat. Even those who traveled between stars to see me fight feared me. My lips twisted into what some might mistake for a smile.

Deep down, they knew what would happen if I got free of the cage and in amongst them, and they feared me. So they should. I didn't know their faces, their names, or even their species—but they paid my captors for this spectacle. That was enough for me to *hate*.

The worst were the journalists, clustering around the cage where they'd get the best angles to watch the fighters die. They made their pay from our suffering and death, and like carrion eaters, they didn't care whose death they feasted on.

I didn't snarl at them. None of them deserved the picture that would make. Except…a flash of red hair at the back of the baying pack caught my eye. Someone new, of a species I didn't recognize, watching me with eyes like green jade and an expression I couldn't place. Not the joy, the hunger, the bloodlust the other journalists shared. Something sad, or maybe angry. Whoever caused it, I felt an instinctive need to slay them and offer the pale-skinned female the offender's heart.

"Tor-**agah**," another chant went up on the far side of the cage, drowning out my fans. "Tor-**agah!**"

My opponent had arrived. With difficulty, I turned away from the intriguing female to face the monster my captors pitted me against. At once, I saw why he had such a loud cheering section. The blue-skinned, scaled monster stood a head taller than me, his eyes burning with an inner rage to mirror my own. A ragged scar ran down his torso, and another marked his neck where someone had come close to tearing out his throat.

In his right hand, he carried a curved sword, its edge honed so sharp it looked like it could cut a god. Somewhere, he'd lost his left arm, only to replace it with a shining chrome cybernetic limb. Clumsy but powerful, it looked like it belonged on an industrial robot, not a person.

This fight might be a challenge. I closed my right fist, activating the electro-gauntlet that was my only weapon, and let go of everything but the fight. For the next few blissful minutes, I was free.

2

ABIGAIL

"This is revenge for me turning you down, isn't it?" I muttered as I pushed my way through the crowd, searching for a good place to view a fight I didn't want to watch. Predictably, the best places had been claimed by journalists who'd gotten in early, so I set my eye on the space behind the crew from *Blood, Guts, and Video*, shrugging my apologies at the annoyed glares of the aliens as I shoved my way past.

"Never," the over-friendly voice of my editor spoke through my implanted comm. "That's all in the past. You were simply the best available asset, and this is a great opportunity."

Yeah, sure. Totally believable. "What makes you think I'm qualified for this, Tony? I don't do sports coverage, let alone illegal blood sports."

He chuckled, an unpleasant sound in person.

Beamed directly into my brain made it about a thousand times worse. "You have the number one qualification in the business, Abigail. You're on the right planet at the right time."

I grumbled under my breath, but that was hard to argue with. Just bad luck for me, and good luck for the agency. Elbowing my way through a group of Akedians with more viciousness than was strictly necessary, I finally reached the space I wanted and looked at the fighting pit itself.

The converted warehouse gave it a brutal, industrial feel, all bare concrete and metal. Crowds filled the space around the pit itself, most of them fans of one fighter or the other, but with a sizeable minority just here to see someone's blood without a care for whose it was. Bookies circulated through the audience, taking last-minute bets, and followed by vendors who offered refreshments and memorabilia to those who fancied paying hundreds of credits for cheaply printed t-shirt designed by someone's ten-year-old child.

In the middle of it all, the cage waited. Thick bars welded together, it looked like overkill, more art than precaution. A way to make the fighters seem more dangerous, and to thrill those in the front row, because no one could break through bars even half that thick.

I'd never admit it worked on me, not anywhere Tony might hear.

At last, I looked at the fighters themselves. Shrouded in mystery, this was the first time I'd seen either of them, and for once I saw an appeal to the event. One fighter, Toragah, was a scaled blue lizard with a metal arm and a shimmering blade, scarred and angry, prowling back and forth. I looked him over, getting a solid record of him before the fight. The other, Gragash, was…

Well, he was stunning. No two ways about it. Green skin covered powerful muscles, and while he stood at least seven feet tall, his shoulders were broad enough that he almost looked stocky. Tusks protruded from the corners of his full, firm lips, adding to the appeal of his chiseled jaw. He wore a scowl that dripped contempt for everything, everyone, around him.

Aside from that scowl, he was kind enough to wear very little. A broad gorget to protect his neck and upper chest, a kilt short enough to show off his powerful thighs, and a gauntlet that crackled with lightning.

He moved like a tiger, graceful and deadly. My stomach filled with butterflies as I watched him, and I caught myself chewing on my lip.

"Oh, so that's your type, hey?" Tony's voice reminded me I really should have killed the camera feed before ogling the fighter, and my cheeks burned. "More into the monster than the man? I guess I should have kept up the karate."

Blinking the code to disable my eyeware cameras, I hissed my reply. "Wouldn't have helped, Tony. I can't imagine a world in which I wouldn't kick your ass in a fight."

Brave words. Probably stupid ones, the sensible voice

in the back of my mind whispered. As usual, she turned up a moment too late for me to act on her advice. I kept myself in good shape, and Tony was more than twice my age, but he was still bigger and meaner than me. I wouldn't bet on myself in a fight.

It shut him up, though, which was the main point. I'd take the immediate victory and worry about consequences later.

Blinking my cameras on again, I tried to work out what fans of the sport would pay to see. I'd have bet my last Credit Imperial that my natural focus would be popular with more fans than they would like to admit, but that wasn't what *Alien Arenas* would pay me for.

The two fighters strode back and forth, glaring at each other impatiently. They wanted the fight over with, both of them straining at invisible leashes and snarling insults at each other. Trash talk; I wished I was close enough to make out the words. The amplified voice of the announcer drowned out everything as she worked the crowd until, at last, they were eager enough for her taste.

A shrill whistle started the fight, and the gladiators leaped at each other, blurs colliding with an impact I felt in my bones. Their attacks came too fast for me to follow, and I just had to hope my camera caught enough of the grisly detail to hold a fight-fan's attention. A few seconds later, the fighters parted, catching their breath and circling.

The Orc warrior left a trail of blood, and his foe moved slower than before—both had taken injuries in their clash. I couldn't tell whose were worse. Their next exchange was more cautious, neither fighter going for the quick kill. They exchanged light, probing blows before the sheer strength of Toragah's mechanical arm forced Gragash back.

My heart was in my throat as I tried to stay focused on the fight, despite the way I winced every time either fighter delivered a solid hit. From the sound the fans made, this was a great show. I forced myself to keep watching, swallowing my horror at what might happen at any moment.

Why do I care what happens to that Orc? I didn't have an answer, just a solid certainty I cared. I had to force open my hands from fists so tight my nails cut into my palms as Toragah drove Gragash back against the cage's bars. The bigger alien's sword blurred, moving too fast to see, and Gragash had nowhere left to run. I froze, staring, and I wasn't the only one. The whole arena fell silent, Toragah's fans with anticipation, Gragash's with dread.

Gragash's back hit the bars, and Toragah thrust without hesitation. Time slowed to a crawl for me as the point of the blade stabbed toward the orc's neck. It was perhaps an inch away when Gragash's lightning-gloved hand struck the sword, sending it past him and between the bars.

Though Toragah must have been surprised, you couldn't tell from his reflexes. He leaped back, withdrawing his blade—or trying to. The orc gladiator smashed his gauntleted fist into the blade, and, caught between his hand and the bars, it snapped. Toragah only kept a couple of inches of steel, looking at the remains of his blade with almost comical confusion. Before he could recover, Gragash had stabbed the rest of the sword up under his chin. Lightning crackled over it.

The silent moment stretched, and then, finally, Toragah fell. Gragash stepped aside, and the giant blue warrior hit the floor of the cage with a thump that broke the crowd's paralysis. All around me, they went wild.

"Abigail, Abigail, those are some amazing shots," Tony said. He sounded no more sincere than before. "You're going to win awards for this."

"There are awards for reporting on illegal sports?"

"Not *officially*, no, but come on. These are gold, and if nothing else, *Alien Arenas* will pay you extra. This is your ticket to the big time, honey. Stick with me, and I'll make you a star reporter."

Sure, except I never want to see anything like that again. Glad as I was that Gragash won, the kill was still a grizzly sight I wouldn't forget in a hurry.

"Don't call me honey, and thanks, but no thanks. Somehow, I think your help comes with a price tag I don't want to pay."

"Aw, don't be like that. We can make a lot of cash together, you know. You got some dynamite shots of *Gragash!* Do you know how rare that is? That fucking Orc never talks to the press, never does photoshoots. When someone manages to get a picture, he always looks like he's about to rip the photographer's head off. But you? You got him looking *sad.*"

The glee with which Tony said that made my skin crawl. *Yeah, wonderful, awesome, I got a photo that shows the killing machine's secret misery.* I shook my head and tried to ignore the creep. At least he wasn't anywhere nearby, so I didn't have to worry about him turning up and wanting to celebrate or something. Then again, he was only in orbit. I'd rather have a few lightyears between us.

He's got a point about the money, though. I got good pics, and the video will be worth something even if I flinched at some of the good bits. I sighed. Money was a powerful motivator, especially given the debt I'd taken on for my implants. When I got them, I'd had starry-eyed dreams of investigative reporting, following shadowy figures, breaking open conspiracies at the heart of the Terran Hegemony. Seeing the galaxy.

Instead, all they got me was a creep in my head and a chance to travel to such delightful spots as…an alien bloodsport arena. Fan-fucking-tastic.

Pictures were one thing, even ones that showed a new side of a pit fighter. But if I'd seen a side of him no one else had, maybe I could snag an interview, too?

Worth a try. And not, I told myself sternly, as an excuse to get closeup shots of his amazing abs.

*Not **just** that, anyway,* a thirsty voice in the back of my mind piped up. *There's also his magnificent ass.*

Telling myself to shut up was unproductive, so instead I rolled my eyes.

3

GRAGASH

The thrill of victory was lacking. In this business, it always was. Standing over the body of my defeated foe, I saw exactly how much our lives were worth. A pair of Baurans emerged from Toragah's entrance, looking at his body with disgust. One kicked the corpse, then spat on it. His companion chattered away in a language I didn't know, but the contempt dripping from his words didn't need translation.

My opponent's 'managers' were unhappy with his performance, which was understandable. Their disrespect towards his remains was not. I felt the snarl spread across my face and stepped forward, lightning crackling across my fist, and the Baurans exchanged worried glances.

"Another splendid victory, Gragash." Ty'anii's voice held an edge of warning, and without looking, I knew the smile the Prytheen female was sporting. More a predator's hungry grimace than anything friendly. With a last snarl at the Baurans, I lowered my arm. Crushing their skulls would not be worth the consequences, so I would have to make do with making them flinch.

Captain Vaher sauntered in behind Ty'anii, looking every bit the dashing pirate captain he wasn't. His long coat billowed like a cloak, and his shirt was open to show off the crimson skin of his chest. If I'd ever harbored any illusions about the romance of space pirate life, Vaher and his crew had cured me of it. To be fair to them, they'd cured me of most romantic ideals I'd held. They were thorough, if nothing else.

While the captain spoke to the Baurans in their own tongue, Ty'anii checked me over for injuries. As always, I hadn't noticed all of them during the fight. That sword had been sharp as anything I'd seen, and fighting a skilled swordsman without taking a few cuts was close to impossible. None of the cuts looked dangerous to me, though.

"Aw, nothing a bit of sprayskin won't fix," she confirmed with a pout. She was the closest thing to a medic Vaher had, and she liked her skills to be useful. Something anyone could fix with a spray can wouldn't remind anyone of her importance. For my part, I was glad I wouldn't end up in her infirmary again.

Vaher finished his business with the Baurans, and we left them to deal with the corpse. Ty'anii finished her examination by manacling my wrists to my belt,

CLAIMED BY THE ORC

and the two of them flanked me, brushing away the various fans and journalists clustering around the exit.

I glared at them as we passed, parasites and sadists all. Vaher and Ty'anii, by contrast, were both all smiles, greeting the regulars as we passed. My angry snarls had no impact—anyone frightened off by them wouldn't hang around to get a picture with me.

My main reason for glaring around was the hope I'd see that mysterious red-haired female again. There was no sign of her among the journalists, though, nor could I see her hanging back in the crowds. I snarled at myself—why was I even bothering? It wasn't as though I'd be able to speak with her.

Journalists threw the usual array of questions at me, and got the usual lack of response in return. Fuck them. I wasn't here to help them make money. Ty'anii hung back to talk to them instead, as usual, and fending off the predictable questions with practiced ease. She had the right presence for the kinds of media that covered these events—pretty, petty, and cruel.

"You ever wonder if your monster there can talk?" one asked once we were through the crowd and heading back aboard the *Darha's Blessing*. He probably thought I could no longer hear him, which told me everything I needed to know about his knowledge of my people. "Most Orcs can, right?"

Ty'anii laughed. "Some can, sure. Big green and stupid here? Doubt it. He'd have told us to go fuck ourselves by now if he could."

With that, she waved and left them behind, rejoined

Vaher and me, and closed the hatch behind her. Vaher grinned at her.

"Hey, don't be too hard on Gragash," he said. Arisrans, like Orcs, had good hearing. "He won us a lot of money today. Maybe we should get him a treat before the next bout."

I shuddered to think what Vaher might have in mind. Hopefully, he'd forget about it just as he did most 'promises' he made to those he considered property.

4

ABIGAIL

The ship Gragash arrived on wasn't hard to locate. *Darha's Blessing* was an old Akedian light hauler, a run-down ship that wouldn't look out of place at one of Earth's spaceports. Bulky and squat, it was mostly cargo space—one central hold running the length of the ship, surrounded by smaller spaces with independent environments for specialist cargo.

Perched on top, the crew quarters were relatively small. Space for a half-dozen cabins at most, with the rest of the space devoted to a pair of blaster cannon crudely welded on. It was too much firepower for any legitimate trader, making the *Blessing* an obvious pirate ship.

What made it obviously the right ship was the mural painted on the hull, an Orc warrior holding a thunderbolt in his raised fist. The likeness of Gragash wasn't perfect, but it was close enough to recognize him.

Whoever had painted it hadn't taken the chance to repaint the second engine, which was a bright yellow where the rest was a dull gray. That wasn't the only sign of poor maintenance choices, either. The edges of its vents were crusted with rust, the hull had dents the size of cars, and someone had haphazardly welded metal plates over the holes where something punched all the way through.

I lowered my gaze to the market that had sprung up on the cracked concrete surface of the spaceport. Like most ships, the *Blessing's* loading ramp was down, and the crew were hawking their ill-gotten wares at its foot. They were busier than most, surrounded by a chaotic mix of aliens all shouting over each other. Fans of Gragash, slavers, traders, all wanted something from the ship's crew, who only seemed interested in talking to the slavers—they had a few aliens in chains to sell, and I winced at the sight. Awful as slavery was, from the run-down look of the *Blessing*, these poor folks were likely to be safer here.

I eased my way through the crowd, careful not to attract attention. Growing up in the remnants of London had trained me well for that, and with the guards distracted, I had no trouble making it to the base of the ramp. That was the point of no return, and I paused to think my plan over one last time.

I'd rather have talked it over with someone, but Tony was the closest thing I had to a friend on the planet, and he hadn't picked up when I called him. If he wondered where I'd gotten to, he'd shown no sign of concern. I wasn't sure why that annoyed me. Did I want his support for my stupid idea, or for him to tell me not to go through with it?

Because the plan *was* stupid. I knew it, but I didn't care. Doing what guys like Tony told me to wouldn't get my career anywhere, and nor would playing it safe. *If I think too long, I'll talk myself out of this,* I told myself. With one last glance to make sure the crew was busy, I ducked under the guardrail and scrambled up the ramp into the *Darha's Blessing's* hold.

I'd half expected to find that the dilapidated outer hull was a cunning ruse, that inside I'd find a well-oiled piracy machine. It was both a relief and a disappointment to find the cargo decks were in even worse condition than I'd suspected. The few working lights flickered as though on the verge of failing, casting eerie shadows in the gloom. In the dim, inconstant light, I saw the sad remains of loot from pirate raids. Mostly luggage, and not high-end stuff. That was easy to sell, unlike this pile of bags stolen from ordinary folks. Rummaged through for anything worth selling, whatever remained they left here.

Somewhere, in amongst the heaps of stolen lives, I heard voices haggling over the cost per pound of the bags. *How fucking desperate are these people?* It seemed such a petty evil, but the *Blessing's* crew seemed determined to wring every cent from their crimes.

I snapped some pictures as I snuck past, on the principle that you never knew what might be important. Maybe, if I got caught, I could pretend to be an interested customer, though how I'd fake enthusiasm for suitcases full of worthless junk was beyond me.

Gragash wasn't in the main hold, I knew that instantly. There would be fans shouting his name if he was that accessible. So either he had one of the crew cabins, or he was in one of the other cargo sections. On the basis that the latter were easier to search without attracting suspicion, I wound my way through the heaps of discarded belongings to the nearest hatch.

A viewer mounted beside it showed a collection of empty slave cages inside. I shuddered at the sight, snapped a few pics for context, and pressed on. All I needed was to find Gragash, grab some pictures, and get a quote out of him. An interview would be better, but I'd had second thoughts about pushing my luck by hanging around and chatting.

I found the next hatch, stopping to stare at the monitor. Where the last slave-hold had been empty, this one was full to bursting. Crowded *with Orcs.*

They looked like teenagers, though I wouldn't have bet on my ability to tell an Orc's age. Three adults led them in some kind of chanting ritual—a prayer, maybe?—but none of them were Gragash. One too old, one too skinny, and one too female.

The only furnishings I could see were heaps of ragged blankets, none of which could have hidden the champion. I cursed under my breath.

"Okay, so they aren't keeping him with the other Orcs," I muttered to myself. "And they're not trying to sell them. What the fuck is this?"

"I've got a better question," a rough voice said behind me, and a heavy hand fell on my shoulder. "Who the fuck are you?"

Instincts born in London alleys had me moving as soon as I knew he was there, but he'd had more experience than any of the lads I'd dodged back on Earth. Too quick for me to escape, his thick fingers clamped onto my shoulder with bruising strength. The elegant dodge-roll I had planned came to an abrupt, painful stop.

Okay, not ideal, but I can salvage this. Deliberately optimistic, I did my best to look professional, sincere, and non-threatening.

"Hey, let go of me." I tried to make that a calm command, but it came out closer to a desperate plea. "Look, I'm press. I'm with *Alien Arenas,* just trying to make a living. You can look through my pics, delete anything you don't want published."

Which is the only reason I carried a camera. My cybernetic eyes took all the photos I wanted, and I could give up the camera without worrying about what I'd lose. Unfortunately, the alien didn't play along with my clever ruse. He ignored everything I said and pulled me back into the center of the hold.

I stumbled along behind him along a narrow path between two walls of stolen cargo. Underfoot, the metal decking creaked as I struggled to pull away. Stains and rust marked the deck as well as the walls, and the cargo was no better. These thugs were making insane amounts of money while spending nothing on maintaining their ship.

A glance at my captor showed where his share of the money went—his clothes dripped with ill-considered finery. Gold chains jangled at his neck, platinum piping down the sleeves of his stained velvet coat, gem-studded piercings on his face. He looked like a man who'd heard of taste, and murdered the person who mentioned it.

"Captain," he called out as we emerged from the cramped cargo hold and into a room set up for the crew's recreation. Three people looked up from a table set with a complicated game featuring holograms, cards, and knives.

The three couldn't have been more different. A portly Akedian who looked like a waxwork left in the summer sun looked around at me, scratching under his silver-gray hair. Across from him lounged two I recognized from the arena. The first was a Prytheen warrior, her blue skin covered in tattoos. And I mean covered: she proved that by wearing gun belts and little else. She curled up against an Arisran male, tall and red-skinned, winding white horns framing a cold, hard face. A demon in the flesh, he peered at me over the papers he'd been reading while the others played.

Those two I recognized from the arena. At least it confirmed I was in the right place.

"What is it, Fenx?" he asked, voice a harsh rasp. Cold eyes flicked across me, assessing and judging. I shivered, my blood suddenly running ice cold. "Where'd you find that?"

"In the cargo hold," my captor said, shoving me forward. "Taking pictures of the Orc, uh, colony. Figured I should ask you before I slit her throat."

The captain's laugh was anything but comforting. "Seems like you've made a mistake, girl. Air costs money, so does food. Got a reason I shouldn't put you out the airlock and save some credits?"

"You've not even taken off yet," I protested. "Just put me ashore now, and I'll give you a glowing review, okay?"

"Ah, so you're press." The Arisran shook his head. "Not a great start, I'll be honest—I value my privacy. What else do you have?"

The Prytheen's narrowed eyes warned me away from a path I had no intention of trying. *Back off,* her look said. *He's **my** meal ticket.*

I wanted to laugh. Like throwing myself at a smuggler, slaver, and crime boss was in any way a good idea, even without a jealous girlfriend in the mix. Laughing at her seemed like an even worse idea, though, so I kept my calm and tried to think.

"If you don't want me to write about you, no problem. I'll write what you want about someone else, keep your name out of it." That had to be worth something, I thought, and the captain's eyes lit up.

"That has potential," he said, stroking his chin. "But how can I be sure you'll go through with it?"

"You can't, boss," the Prytheen interjected. "She'd say anything to keep herself alive."

What the fuck's your problem, lady? It didn't help that she was right. I'd make the deal happily, but only to get out alive. Once I was away from the pirates? Fuck these guys.

Before I could figure out a way to convince him, an unpleasant, predatory grin spread across her features. "But you know what? You promised Gragash a treat, and you know how much he hates journos. I think he'll enjoy tearing her limb from limb, and it'll save a day or two of food rations for him. Keeping him fed is expensive."

The captain's smile was ice cold as he nodded once, quick and decisive. "Fenx, Brish, take her upstairs and throw her to the Orc."

HE WASN'T in the cargo holds at all. Fenx, the asshole wearing all the gold, dragged me up into the crew levels of the ship, now accompanied by the Akedian, who had to be Brish. Neither answered my questions, and when I tried to pull away, Brish pulled a shock-prod from his belt. The crackle of energy when he activated it put a stop to my thoughts of escape.

Perhaps it's all an act? If they're keeping him up here, in an officer's cabin, maybe the brutal barbarian is a stage persona? I almost laughed at the idea, and at the image it conjured. Gragash, mighty Orc warrior, lounging around a luxurious room wearing a smoking jacket and puffing on a pipe. Not speaking to anyone in public because he wasn't able to hide his posh accent.

I wished I could believe it, but no. Even before we reached the hatch, I knew fate wouldn't be so kind.

Battered out of shape, fist-sized dents marked the metal, making the hatch squeal as Fenx slid it open. The dents came from *inside*, and looking at the inch-thick steel of the hatch, I shivered at the strength that must have taken. What lay beyond just added to the icy fear running through my veins.

The stateroom was, for a spaceship, huge. Big enough that shadows hid most of it, the light spilling past us the only source of illumination other than the distant stars beyond a viewport. This had to be the owner's cabin, or perhaps the *Blessing* once carried wealthy passengers from star to star. The walls were a sumptuous shade of purple, though often discolored by fire or blood. Luxurious furnishings made from genuine wood—I could tell from the broken remnants of what remained of a bed—lay in pieces, piled up against the wall. My feet sank into a soft carpet, thicker than some mattresses I'd slept on.

A few steps into the room, heavy metal bars blocked our way. Crudely welded, thick as my wrist, they stretched floor-to-ceiling and wall-to-wall, turning most of the stateroom into a cell capable of holding a monster. The only break in the cage was a barred door set into them.

My captors both hesitated before approaching the bars, though there was no sign of life in the gloom beyond. Heart racing, I held back too, only for Fenx to shove me roughly against the cold iron of the bars.

"Wake up, Gragash. The captain has a treat for you." Brish ran his shock-prod back and forth along the bars, clattering loud enough to wake the dead. Inside the cell, *something* moved.

I heard it more than saw it, the *clink* of chains shifting, a creak as the Orc's weight shifted. My captors stepped back from the cage at once. A shadow moved in the gloom, barely visible but *huge*. In the arena, Gragash looked big. Now I realized I'd underestimated his size.

"Stop fucking around," the Fenx hissed at his companion, and I had to agree. Why rile up the monster? "Let's get her in there and us out of here."

Okay, that I didn't agree with so much, but they wouldn't listen to my comments. Brish waved his hand over the cage's lock and the barred door swung open. Quick as a flash, Fenx shoved me inside and slammed the door behind me. The lock engaged with a forbidding *clunk*, and there I was, trapped in a cage with the monster I'd been stupid enough to want to interview.

Well, fuck it. Nothing to lose trying to get it now. "Mr. Gragash?"

The answering growl sent a shiver through me, and I stepped back. Or tried to—the bars stopped me going even a step, the steel ice-cold through my clothes. Gragash shifted his weight again, looming in the darkness, and I tried to pull myself back into the light.

My captors laughed behind me, but I heard the edge of fear in their voices. Swallowing, I wondered what they expected to happen, what made those hardened criminals afraid.

"Get. Out." Gragash's voice was deep, impossibly deep, and laced with deep-set rage. Nothing human could make that sound. It vibrated through me, hitting me hard and taking my breath away.

Scary? Yes, absolutely, of course. Also hot enough to melt through steel. I bit my lip, squirming back against the bars. Beyond them, the gangsters fled the room. I barely noticed them go, but I did notice the hatch grinding shut again, leaving me in a stateroom-cage lit only by starlight.

Without the outside lighting, my cybernetic eyes adjusted faster than normal human eyes do. The shadowy figure lurking in the dark took on depth and form, and I swallowed nervously as Gragash took a step forward. He loomed over me like a mountain of green muscle, burning eyes glaring deep into my soul. I'd seen him fight from a distance, but nothing had prepared me for just how big he was up close. Tall, and broad-shouldered even for his height, with muscles that would have been grotesque on anyone smaller. On his frame, though, they looked perfect.

Tusks protruded from his strong-jawed face, his lips curling into a hungry smile as he looked at me.

Eyes raked up and down me, pausing at my breasts, my hips. My skin warmed wherever he looked, and I felt a flush creep across my cheeks.

Unbidden, my gaze wandered down his body. His bare chest, rising and falling as he breathed deep. The perfect six-pack of his abs. Thank god, he wore a kilt of dark leather, but the size of the bulge under it me shudder. If that muscle was as big as the rest of them...

"I..." Swallowing, I tried again. "I'm Abigail Harkness, and I'm here to—"

He cut me off, voice hard and harsh. "Here to play games. I am Gragash, and I do not *play*."

5

GRAGASH

The human flinched at my hard tone, but didn't react as the females usually did. The urd'ash who kept me as their slave had brought females, and a few males, to see me. Rich tourists, blood hot from watching me fight, who wanted to bed the victor and go home with a scandalous tale to tell.

I had no interest in being the brute that they giggled about with their friends. Their oh-so-daring escapade, the crazy adventure of their youth.

All of them either fled, too frightened to go through with it in person, or flung themselves at me. I preferred the former response; it saved me having to pick them up and throw them out of my cage. They were not for me.

This was different. The human wasn't here for some cheap thrill, and she hadn't paid to be in my presence. She was here against her will, and the urd'ash were aware of how much I hated the journalists who followed me. They'd sent her here to die, and she knew it.

Her scent filled the air—fear and excitement, sweat and smoke, a dizzying treat for an Orc. I drew a deep breath, tasting her arousal on the air, and saw her shiver. Despite her desire, she wasn't here to use me as a plaything. She feared me, but not with the mindless terror that drove others to flee my presence. The human was something altogether different from my previous 'guests.'

I stepped closer, looming over her, and her breath caught. I hadn't seen many humans close up, but I could see at a glance that this one was special. Intense eyes looked back at me, green with golden flecks, framed by dark lashes. Freckles dusted her strange, pale skin, and red hair cascaded down her back like a waterfall of fire. The curves of her body called out to be touched, explored, devoured, and the coverings she wore only made me want to rip them off her to see the skin beneath. A black t-shirt with a logo I didn't recognize, strategically ripped black pants made of some tough fabric, and heavy boots. They looked good on her. They'd look better *off* her.

"What are you, human?" I asked, snarling my question in her face. "Why are you in my cage?"

She stammered something in a language I didn't know, then switched to galtrade. "Hi, I'm Abigail Harkness, and I'm here to interview you? I'm a freelance journalist."

Something about the way she said it made me

laugh, a bark of amusement that made the human flinch back against the bars of my cage. The earnest confidence of her words was at odds with her fear, but not dishonest. I'd learned the taste of lies, and this was not one.

Was it aspirational? Not true *yet,* but she hoped it would be? If so, I both envied her belief in a better future, and pitied her for it. Hope was a sweet poison, one that I had long ago purged from my system.

"You are here as a reward for me," I said, correcting her. "A toy. So the urd'ash told me."

A delightful blush spread across her pale cheeks and she glanced back over her shoulder before answering. "Okay, yes, that's what Vaher said. But it's not why I came aboard, and I've got no intention of being *anyone's* toy. So, how about an interview?"

"You are in no position to decide that, human. Slavers caught you. You are theirs. It is pointless to argue."

Her eyes narrowed, her blush brightened, and she bared her teeth. "I'm not arguing. I don't need to. They don't get to say what I am unless I let them. They don't get to decide what you are, either. Fuck that."

Her earnest expression, her passion, her resilience, all reminded me too much of the orc I'd once been. So certain I could fight my way out of any trap, only to be caught in the web of deceit Captain Vaher wove around me. I'd lost that certainty along the way, long years of hopeless captivity dimming its flame, but

Abigail's was still strong, and bright enough to revive some of my own.

Fuck Vaher, and fuck them all. I am still Gragash, and my foes will not define me.

Perhaps some of that young orc still lived deep in me.

"We are not what they say we are," I agreed. "We make our own choices."

She nodded shakily, her breath caught, and I heard her heart race. Predators at heart, orcish senses have always been keen, but this was different. More. I was aware of Abigail and everything about her in a way I'd never felt before.

I leaned in, close enough to feel the heat radiating from her, close enough to whisper.

"And I know what you want me to choose, little human."

6

ABIGAIL

I thought I was going mad. Gragash loomed over me like a green cliff of muscle and raw masculinity, his voice a rumbling whisper that shook me to my core. Slavers had thrown me to him like a bone to their favorite dog, and despite that, god, I was so thirsty for him.

His hand, massive and heavy, rested next to my head. So close, I understood why our captors worried about him tearing his way out of a cage. His arms were like tree trunks, if the trees had spent a lot of time lifting weights. The wall of his green chest in front of me made me squirm. Yes, he'd trapped me, but was an improvement in every way to being in the hands of his captors.

It was the smell, though, that really drove me insane. His scent was heavy, musky, earthy, and it touched something deep inside me. Some kind of primal drive responded to Gragash's presence, his scent, and *ohmygod* his words.

I cannot believe I'm considering going along with this. Pirates had thrown me to their gladiator-slave as a reward for winning a fight, and I was about to cooperate?

Nuh-uh, you don't get to talk yourself out of this. My inner voice was infuriatingly reasonable in its horniness. *This **is** different. He's not just grabbed me to have his way with me, he's giving me a choice, and that changes everything.*

I was trapped, pinned against the cage by his mighty body. His face next to mine, the heat of his body radiating against me, hot breath washing over my neck. He said I wanted him, and I couldn't call it a lie. But he hadn't touched me, not yet, and I was sure he wouldn't —not until I gave permission.

Though if I gave permission, I didn't expect to get a say in what happened afterward. Gragash's dominant energy rolled off him like waves, and the thought of surrendering to him sent a shiver through me.

The heat radiated from him and intensifying as he leaned in ever closer. Not quite touching me, but so close my skin prickled. "You want this," he said with an unshakeable confidence entirely different from Tony's arrogance. "You want me. And I want you."

As he spoke, he ran a single fingernail up my side, lifting my t-shirt and teasing the skin beneath.

"Before you agree, you should know—I am an orc. I will not be gentle with you." He paused and lowered his voice to a whisper I could barely hear. "Nor will you want me to be."

I licked my lips, looked up into his dark, intense eyes, and my heart skipped a beat as I spoke, managing only a single word. "Yes."

His response was faster than I'd thought possible. He grabbed me and lifted me against the bars, putting my face level with his. He brought his mouth to my neck, tusks grazing my skin, and I gasped. He chuckled darkly as I squirmed.

Every nerve in my body was on fire with desire for this orc, and I blushed to hear myself moan aloud. As if that was a signal, he stepped back, put me down on unsteady feet, and bared his sharp teeth in a predatory grin.

"Undress," he said, no, commanded. His eyes flashed as I obeyed without pausing to think, pulling my t-shirt over my head and throwing it aside. My bra followed just as fast. I unbuckled my belt and kicked off my boots before pausing and turning to Gragash. He stared at me with a fierce intensity, as though he was committing every inch of my skin to memory.

In turn, I watched him undo the buckle holding his kilt closed, letting the leather garment fall to the floor. There was nothing underneath, of course. Just orc. So very much orc.

Very *hard* orc.

My jaw fell open at the sight, and I whimpered. His cock stood hard and proud, dark green veins coiling around it, the head glistening with pre-cum. It was enormous, scarily big, too big? Part of my brain insisted no human could take that emerald monster.

I licked my lips and knew that I had to try. For science.

"Did I tell you to stop?" Gragash rumbled, and I unfastened my jeans and slid them down, taking my panties with them and leaving myself as naked as he was.

He took another long look at me, slowly tracing my curves, and I fought my urge to cover myself. My cheeks burned, the flush spreading down and across my breasts as he admired me.

"Come here," he said at last, an unmistakable crack of command in his tone. To my surprise, I moved before my mind processed the order. *What is this? Some kind of psychic power?*

I knew better. It was just *Gragash*, his hunger for me and his confidence and his sheer dominance.

His hand slid into my hair, gently but firmly pulling me with him as he withdrew into the shadows at the back of his cell. Even my eyes didn't adjust to this darkness, and he faded from my view. Like the Cheshire Cat, his smile was the last thing to go, teeth and tusks reflecting what little light reached this far. With his free hand, Gragash teased his way across my breasts, his clawed fingertips adding a delicious touch of danger where they scraped over my tender skin. My nipples, hardening at his touch, sent little bursts of pleasure through me as he played.

It didn't seem like *he* had any trouble with the dark. Even blind, I refused to let him have all the fun.

Rather than fumble in the darkness, I raised my hands to my head, found his wrist, and stroked up the inside of his arm, digging my nails in just enough to draw a growl. That deepened as my hands reached his chest and I stroked my nails down over his nipples, a mirror of his movements.

His breath hitched and a tremor coursed down both his arms. *Oh, sensitive, are we?* I smiled and tweaked his right nipple. His hand tightened in my hair, not enough to hurt, but enough to make it clear it *could.*

"Careful, little one," he rumbled, and his warning tone did something to me. "You don't want to test me."

Of course not. Why would I? What could I possibly gain by annoying him? It would be a stupid idea.

So, obviously, I tweaked his left nipple harder. What can I say? I have a self-destructive streak.

Gragash responded with the reflexes of a gladiator, and I couldn't follow what happened in the next half-second. All I know is, I started it standing up, everything blurred, and then I was on my hands and knees with Gragash behind me. One of his hands was still in my hair, the other on my hip, and his cock slid along the crack of my ass. I moaned and pressed back into him, unable to even pretend to struggle or resist.

Gragash rumbled a pleased sound, slipping the hand on my hip around, his fingers parting my slick folds. "Mmm, such an eager little one," he whispered at my eager writhing. "*Good* girl."

My breath caught at those two little words, and I bit my lip to stifle a moan. Gragash did *not* need to know how that affected me.

A futile effort when my body betrayed me, and his hungry growl told me he was well aware. As he slid a finger into me, he kissed my neck, tusks digging almost painfully into my skin and making me shiver. His hand in my hair kept me in place, helpless and under his control.

I pressed back against him, wriggling, trying to tease him as he teased me. It worked, or at least his cock stiffened even further. I swallowed, and wondered if making that shaft bigger was really a good idea.

My heart pounded, and I whimpered wordlessly as he pulled back, breaking contact between me and his dick for just a second. Whimpered again, louder, when he pressed himself back to me, the head of his monster rubbing against my opening. *Too big,* part of me cried. But my body didn't agree, and the pulsing *need* in my core called out to be filled.

His first thrust buried him deep inside me, driving me down into the blankets. My body stretched around him, took him deeper than I'd thought possible, and *my god,* it felt amazing.

The second thrust pushed him even deeper, his rough hands pulling back to meet his thrust. I yelled out at the third, my voice muffled by the blankets. Each time he withdrew, I felt an aching void inside me.

With every thrust, he filled that void, a wave of pleasure crashing through my body. I cried out as he fucked me with a brutal passion, the waves coming closer and closer together until my world exploded with ecstasy. My body shook wildly and I would have collapsed if Gragash hadn't held me up.

He hadn't finished with me yet.

I tried to speak, though I have no idea what I wanted to say. It didn't matter. Gragash drove the air from my lungs with another forceful thrust, and I felt his cock *thrum* inside me. That made me clench around him, gripping his pulsating rod tighter, and his deep groan told me how he enjoyed that.

His thrusts came faster, harder, more powerful. Each one made me gasp and drove me closer to the edge. Gragash's breathing came faster, his control waning, and I knew he was getting close, too. He hardened even further inside me, his vibrating orc cock drove me wild, and I tried to return the favor by squeezing him inside me. All control lost, Gragash was a wild animal, pounding me into the blankets and biting down hard on my shoulder as his cock twitched —and then unleashed inside me.

His roar of triumph merged with my hoarse scream of pure pleasure as the tidal wave of our shared orgasm carried us away.

7

GRAGASH

Until that night, I had not realized how empty my nest felt. Now, with the human female curled up against me, it seemed a miracle that I'd survived alone for so long. I cradled her against me, listening to her slow breathing and looking down at her.

Asleep, she was even more beautiful. The tense wariness that cloaked her had faded, left me with an utterly relaxed female to hold and protect. *And I **will** protect you, Abigail Harkness, though I do not yet know how.*

Abigail stirred gently, as though to acknowledge my vow. Her fine, fair skin made a delicious contrast to the green of my own, especially where she wrapped her hands around my arm and held on tight. As though she was afraid I'd be gone when she awoke.

I stroked her hair, muttering soothing words to reassure her and marveling at the bright, soft glory of her mane. She had nothing to fear from me. I'd never abandon a sleeping female—and even if I were that kind of urd'ash who *would*, I could not. The cage my captors had locked us in was spacious, but not enough to let us avoid each other.

Darha's Blessing's lights followed the day/night cycle of a planet, and while I'd smashed every light I could, some near the door remained out of my reach. The room slowly brightened, though we remained deep in shadow. Abigail scrunched up her face and tried to burrow her face into my chest to avoid the fake dawn. The sight was adorable and amusing.

"...*laughing* at me," she complained when I chuckled.

"Only a little," I said, and lifted her chin gently. Her aggrieved pout vanished as I kissed her, and her eyes flickered open.

She looked confused but delighted, and her hands roamed my chest and teased me. My body responded at once, and it was her turn to chuckle, though her cheeks burned bright red.

"Well, *good* morning," she said, slipping one hand down to my cock as it stiffened. I gasped, my breath caught, as she slid her fingers around my cock head. The pulse of joy that sent through me made me arch under her. "Ready to go again, are we?"

Her voice barely trembled, though her blush gave away her embarrassment. As much as she wanted me, she wasn't used to this kind of talk. I felt the wicked smile spread over my face, enjoying her shyness as much as her touch. "You are such a delightful, beautiful, sexy girl, Abigail. How could I *not* be ready for more?"

CLAIMED BY THE ORC

She blushed brighter, mumbling something inaudible, and continued to stroke my hardening cock. As she did so, she ducked her head to kiss her way across my chest. I shuddered as she reached my nipples, her pink tongue darting out to flick them.

With a little shiver of her own, she kissed her way downward. Down across my stomach, my abs. Her eyes gleamed when she looked back up at me, and my cock twitched in her hands.

"Turn about," she said, "is fair play."

I would have answered, but she stole my voice by licking her way up my cock, slipping the head into the delightful warmth of her mouth. Swirling her tongue around me, she groaned, the vibrations sending pulses of pleasure through me. It was like nothing I'd ever felt, nothing I'd ever known. And I wanted *more.*

I slid my hand into her magnificent mane of red hair, guiding my human lover down onto me. At first, her response was tentative, then eager as she felt my pleasure building.

"Good girl," I whispered. Abigail shuddered and moaned. "Such a good girl."

The words were like magic, and she took more of me into her hungry mouth each time. Her breath came faster, and I lay back, pressing my fingers between her legs as she curled against me. She spread them wide, her whimpers and sending delicious sensations through me as I sought to return the favor.

Together, we climbed towards a world-shattering

climax, our bodies wrapped around each other, our rhythms synchronized.

I threw my head back, roaring loud, and Abigail bucked against me as I came again, my hot seed flooding her mouth. When I looked back down, she met my gaze with a bright blush and a grin that I could live off for days. She held me tight as she panted, and we both recovered from a second mind-blowing orgasm.

"That was..." she trailed off, and I nodded gravely.

"It was more than words can carry. My words, at least." I was never a poet, and never regretted it more than at that moment. "Anything I say will sound tawdry compared to the experience."

"Yeah." Abigail lay back in the nest of blankets and cushions and scraps of torn mattress, blowing an errant lock of hair out of her face. Relaxed and at peace, she radiated happiness and I basked in her glow while it lasted.

It wasn't long before reality crept back in. Her eyes flicked to the cage bars and back, her neck muscles tightened, and a guarded look settled on her face, as though she'd taken off a mask for a time and now put it back on. My heart sank at the sight, but it was no surprise. In her arms, I'd felt free for the first time in years, but we could only hold reality at bay for so long. The bars at the front of the room were too obvious a reminder of our status aboard the *Blessing*.

I wasn't ready to go back to being a prisoner, though, so I looked for something to distract her.

Something other than the obvious—we couldn't keep away our troubles by fucking, no matter how tempting the idea was.

"What did you want to ask me?" I tried to keep my tone light.

Abigail looked at me and frowned, raising an eyebrow. I tried again. "You wanted to interview me when you arrived. It would be churlish of me to deny you that now."

Her expression cleared, a blush creeping across her cheeks as a smile spread on her lips. "That's not how this works. Sleeping with a source isn't an ethical way to get a story, Gragash."

"Hah. No, I suppose not, but still. Ask your questions." I returned the smile and watched her blush deepen. "I make no promises to give good answers."

"That's more honest than most interviewees," she said, focusing more intently on me. "Um. You should probably put something on, or I'm going to be too distracted to work."

"Fine." I pulled my kilt back on, enjoying her eyes as she tracked my every movement. She controlled her expression well, but the flash of disappointment when I covered myself was still visible.

Now that she had her interview, she didn't seem to know what to do with it. We sat across from each other in silence, her eyes roaming the room then snapping back to me, until she blurted out a question.

"What happened to the room?" she asked. "Why do

you have the best room on the ship, and why is it such a wreck?"

I growled. "Vaher gave me this room as a bribe. I am not in a position where I could refuse, so instead, I trashed it. I will not have him place me under an obligation, nor even think he has."

Abigail blinked at that. "You ruined your own bedroom out of spite?"

"Not how I see it," I said, shrugging. "Vaher wants to pretend we have a deal, that he's my manager not the slaving urd'ash he is. If I accept his gifts, I accept some of that claim. Besides, I am an orc! I prefer this nest to the 'civilized' finery he offered me."

"It has its advantages," she admitted. "That sounds like a fine line to tread, though. If you can't refuse his gifts, why does he let you break them?"

"A game. It's all a game to him." I snarled, anger choking my words. Abigail didn't flinch, instead she leaned forward. Someone who didn't fear my rage was a strange novelty, even other orcs would be on guard. Not Abigail, though. I liked that. "He needs me to fight for him, so there are limits to what he can do. So he tries to bribe me, win my compliance. Rejecting them outright would challenge his authority, but breaking them? That's just my 'barbarian ways.'"

"Hang on. Was I another bribe?" Abigail sounded uncertain.

"Yes." I answered honestly. "A clever one, too. He knows how I feel about the journalists who follow the underground fighting circuit like carrion-eaters feasting on the blood of the dead."

"No, don't hold back, tell me how you really feel," Abigail muttered under her breath, too quiet for most to hear. I chuckled, and her cheeks reddened. Her embarrassment only made it funnier, and getting my laughter under control was difficult.

"It's not like this is the work I wanted to do, but I have to pay the bills somehow," she said, a little defensively. "I'm supposed to be an investigative journalist, uncovering corruption and such. Not writing breathless commentary on illegal fights for *Alien Arenas* and the like."

"I suppose that would be better, though I don't think it would change anything," I told her. "I only see those second kind of journalists at the fights, and all they want is meat for their readers. Parasites living off the fighters' suffering and death. Worse, they make it sound exciting and *fun.*"

I spat the last word, realizing I'd bared my teeth and the muscles in my neck were taut enough to vibrate. I unclenched my fists, took a deep breath, and let it out slowly, calming my mind and body.

Abigail watched, eyes wide but unafraid, which helped me get control of my emotions. She rested a hand on my arm while calmly waiting for me to recover.

"I apologize," I said when I trusted myself to speak again.

"Shush. You've every right to be angry at the people

who sell your pain as sport. And you had no idea I wasn't the same as the rest of them." Her gaze dropped from mine. "Hell, I *was*. I came to the fight to report on it like they did. If anyone should apologize, it's me."

I stared at her. Drew a breath to object. Abigail raised a hand to my mouth, silencing me. "We can go on saying sorry to each other for ever, or we can accept each other's apologies and move on. I vote for option two, please. And, um, do you have a shower or something in this mess?"

8

ABIGAIL

I don't know what I expected, but it wasn't the forest grove I found behind the bathroom door. Gragash's low chuckle behind me made me snap my mouth shut, trying not to show my shock. Too late, of course.

The room looked huge, big enough that it had to be fake, but the illusion was so well crafted I couldn't spot the boundary between real and hologram. Discrete lighting guided the eye to the fixtures, and pleasant birdsong filled the air.

A waterfall tumbled down to the rocks next to a pool. Alien plants surrounded it, vines padding the edge, blossoms floating in the water. After the chaotic wreckage of the rest of the suite, it came as a complete surprise.

"You said you trashed everything," I said, stepping forward and running my fingers through the leaves of the nearest tree. Until I touched them, they looked real, but where I made contact, they shimmered and faded out of existence. Holograms this good were expensive to produce. I frowned, looking back at the orc. "You refused to accept any gifts."

Gragash growled, a strange combination of frustration and amusement. "I could claim that destroying something this beautiful would be evil, even if it is a false gift from my enemy. Maybe it's even true, but it's not why this room survived. It's simply hard to wreck. The hologram projectors are behind the walls, and the walls are solid ceramsteel. I did my best, to no effect."

Laughter bubbled up inside me at his earnest explanation. I did my best to control it. "It's too *fake* for you to break?"

Glower intensifying, he bared his tusks in a snarl. "You try punching a hologram, see how it works out for you."

There was just enough of a twinkle in his eye to show he wasn't entirely serious. "Besides, if I destroy everything Vaher gives me, I'm as much under his control as if I accept all the gifts. He'd just start sending me things he wants gone."

"You mean, like he sent you a journalist?"

Am I only alive because Gragash is petty? Not a cheerful thought, but the orc laughed and shook his head. "Little human, you are alive because I would rather gnaw off my arm than see you hurt. From the moment I laid eyes on you, I knew our fates were bound together."

Heat rose in my cheeks, and I had to look away. I

mumbled an incoherent objection, but Gragash wasn't letting me get away with that.

"You may not believe in fate," he said, stepping forward and lifting me off my feet. "I know better. We'll *not* waste our time debating destiny or other questions better put to a priest. We have more valuable things to do."

I squirmed in his grip, though I knew I'd no chance to pull free. He didn't hold me for long, anyway—as soon as he finished speaking, he *threw* me.

My squeal of outrage and terror filled the room, and I flailed as I sailed through the air. A moment later, I hit the pool at the waterfall's base with a stinging splash. Warm water closed over me and I thrashed my way back to the surface, spluttering and glaring.

"I'll get you for that, you fucker." My outraged shout might have been more convincing if I didn't look like a drowned rat, but Gragash wouldn't have taken my threat any more seriously. He was already in the air, leaping into the pool with all the style and elegance of a brick thrown through a window.

Waves from his impact crashed over me, leaving me spluttering again. Folding my arms, I glared at him when he resurfaced, but found it an impossible expression to hold. A smile tugged at my lips and after a few seconds of struggling to suppress it, I gave up. Gragash grinned back at me, unrepentant.

"I'm serious about getting my revenge," I warned him.

"You would disappoint me if you weren't," the orc

said. "Not that I'll make it easy for you. Now relax, little human. This is our haven, and I will not tolerate serious talk here."

The temptation to ask 'Or what?' was strong, and my blush returned to full force at the thought of what his answer might be. I shook off the idea—I didn't want to provoke him, no matter how much fun his response might be. He was right. We had an oasis of peace and calm here, which we should treasure. Even so, I couldn't quite leave the serious topics alone.

"Why do you go along with Vaher's bullshit? I mean, if you tried to escape, you might not make it, but you'd have a chance?"

He sighed and grimaced, answering in a lower tone. "Because it's not just me. Vaher has my kin, and their comfort rests on my behavior. If I go too far, he will sell them to the worst buyers he can find, or just kill them outright. I am not even certain they are still alive. Vaher shows me recorded messages. Recordings are easy to fake."

As soon as he mentioned his kin, I felt an icy stab into my heart. This wasn't a better topic, obviously, and I should have kept my mouth shut. But since I'd already fucked up, at least I could do to something to help.

Raising my hand above the water, palm up, I opened my media library and scrolled back through the images I'd captured until I got to the orcs kept in the hold below. The picture hung above my hand, a shimmering hologram, and I rotated it to show Gragash what I'd seen.

"I took this just before they caught me," I said. Gragash stared as I played the few seconds I'd captured, and a smile spread over his face. With the gentlest touch I'd felt from him yet, he took my hand and lifted it, looking into the hologram image.

"Jarchess," he said, voice so low it was a whisper. "My sister. Yes, that is them. My clan, still alive and together. Still aboard this ship."

Bending, he planted a delicate kiss on my palm. "Thank you, Abigail. You have given me a gift of great value, and I shall not forget that."

My face heated. "It's not that valuable, they're still prisoners and—"

He looked up and met my gaze, silencing me. "They are alive," he repeated. "Together, and in reach. I had almost given up hope."

9

GRAGASH

We emerged from the bathroom grove dripping wet and laughing together, my smile broad and my step lighter than I could remember it. The forest pool had been a valuable escape for me when I was alone. With Abigail to share it, the pain cleared from my soul. And the news that my kin still lived, that Vaher had kept his word, was a bright light in the darkness. It was hope.

A temporary effect, alas, and one that faded when I saw who waited for us beyond the bars of my cage. Captain Vaher leaned against the door, flicking through holographic documents that floated in front of him. As soon as we entered, he banished them with a swipe of his hand and grinned at me.

I think he intended it as a friendly expression, but all it achieved was to remind me I hated this man. More, now that he had threatened my mate. I snarled in return, which he took in his stride. Whatever else he was, Vaher wasn't easy to frighten. Whether that was from courage or stupidity, I didn't speculate.

"Still having fun with your new toy, I see?" he said, nodding to Abigail. "I didn't think she'd survive the night, but it doesn't matter. You enjoy her in your own time, and don't worry, when you break her, we'll get you another."

Abigail, face redder than I'd yet seen, dived under a blanket. A moment later, her face poked out, shooting a glare in Vaher's direction. She didn't speak, which was probably smart, but I saw it eat at her. My human was not one for hiding her feelings.

"You did not come here to tell me what to do with my female," I growled, refusing to cover myself. That would give him the satisfaction of believing he'd discomforted me. "Nor to congratulate me on my win again. So why are you here? To what do I owe this... pleasure?"

There was nothing peasant about it, but I didn't want to give him any reason to be angry. After all, he'd found a new weapon to use against me.

"Ah, young love." Despite his words, his grin would have looked at home on a predator ready to pounce. It lacked even the smallest measure of kindness or friendship. "I remember what it's like being unable to take your eyes, or hands, off a partner. No wonder you're keen to get me out of here, old friend, but you needn't worry. We need to discuss your next fight, which won't take up much of your valuable time."

I was used to swallowing Vaher's false friendship,

though I preferred his crew's more open hostility. This time, it stuck in my craw. The captain narrowed his eyes, sensing my anger.

"Hey, tall, red, and ugly, lay off him." I blinked, as did Vaher. Wrapped in her blanket, Abigail glared, making no attempt to hide her anger. "Gragash made you a fortune, and you owe him everything. In return, you could at least be honest about his status."

"Ms. Harkness, please have a care." Vaher's voice was warm, friendly, and fake. "You're a guest here, and you seem to enjoy your present accommodations. I can always move you to a less comfortable room."

I growled at that, muscles tensing as I measured the distance to him in my mind. Pointless, with the bars between us. The pirate captain was neither stupid nor careless, and he stood outside my reach.

Watching me, measuring my reaction as carefully as I measured his position. I couldn't help feeling I'd given away too much. No fixing that, though. All I could do was change the subject, and hope he hadn't seen as much as I feared. He wouldn't hesitate to use Abigail as a tool against me, as he already used my clan.

"Who am I up against, and where?" Perhaps if I focused on the specifics of his plans and how I'd be useful to him would serve as a distraction.

The captain clapped his hands gleefully, all our disagreements apparently forgotten. "Your last fight put your reputation over the top, Gragash. You're in the big leagues now! Three nights on Lachrin Station. Two low-key fights, easy wins, just to show you off to the paying customers. But the last one, that's a champion's match. A death match pitting you against Korsar, the Guild champion. He's tough, no doubt, but I have every confidence in you."

His eyes twinkled with humor and avarice. "Now, I'll let you get back to your…exercises. You have two days to prepare."

Nowhere near enough time for serious preparations. But then, being locked in here with Abigail meant I'd get a *lot* of exercise in. I'd make do somehow.

10

ABIGAIL

"So, I'm *your* female now, huh?" I asked, hands on my hips, as soon as the hatch closed behind Captain Demon-Face. "You're feeling pretty confident, aren't you?"

"Yes." His answer could have sounded arrogant, but not from Gragash. He was simply answering my question, with sparkling eyes as he saw my surprise. "You are mine, and you know it. You knew it as soon as we met. And I am yours, in turn. No need to play games."

I'd had dates try to claim something from me, of course. Who hasn't? Usually it's the simple 'he paid for dinner, so I owe him a fuck.' Sometimes it's weirder, and I've had a couple of 'you owe me marriage' offers.

Never, not once, had I considered giving in to those claims. Usually, I blocked the asshole's number and forget about them. Gragash's offer was the first I'd considered playing along with.

No, more than that. I wanted to *agree* with him. I *wanted* to be his.

Nope, can't say that! Change the subject, quick.

"Lachrin Station's bad news," I told Gragash, jumping on the first topic that came to mind. "It's a Guild station, and they're used to hosting much worse things than an illegal deathmatch or three. They run it as a luxury resort for bored, decadent, rich assholes, so either this isn't as big a deal as Vaher's pretending, or there's more to it. Blood on the sands won't impress anyone there."

"How did you learn so much about this place?" Gragash asked, still glowering at the hatch. I chuckled ruefully.

"I'd planned on doing an expose on it. Some Terran Hegemony officials are getting wined and dined out there, and probably up to more sketchy stuff."

His brow furrowed, Gragash paced back and forth. I watched him go, trying to dredge up helpful information, until he rounded on me. "Why did you not pursue that story? It is far above some pit fighting reviews."

That's what he's puzzling over? Not how he can escape, not what this means for him? He wants to know about my life. That shouldn't have surprised me, but it did. "The problem was, I had no way in. I applied for a few jobs there, but never even got an interview. I don't have the experience for any of the management positions, and I don't exactly have the looks for a front-of-house job at a galaxy-class vice den."

Gragash's head snapped round at that, and he

moved so fast it almost convinced me he could teleport. One second, he was at the far end of his lair from me. The next, he had me pinned with the bars at my back and his face inches from mine, a furious frown darkening his expression.

"Who told you that?" He demanded an answer with a snarl that would frighten off a tiger. I stammered something, words without meaning, and he cut me off sharply. "What fool, what wretch, thought that *you* would not be the most beautiful attraction at any den of vice you blessed with your presence?"

My mouth dropped open, my heart pounding, and I tried to come up with an answer. My mind spun in circles, dredging up pointless, painful memories. "I… they…"

"They are *wrong,* Abigail ko'Gragash Harkness. Whoever they are, they are as wrong as it is possible to be.

"Your hair is a beautiful firefall, glorious to look upon, magnificent to stroke.

"Your face? Perfection. Eyes that give me insight into your soul, lips that promise heaven in a kiss and deliver it wrapped around my cock.

"Your skin, soft and smooth," he kissed my neck, tusks scratching just enough to make me moan. "A delight to look at, a joy to kiss. Your blush, so expressive, showing the world your passion and need and longing."

I doubt I've ever blushed deeper. And Gragash wasn't done yet.

"Your magnificent breasts, a joy to touch, kiss, bite," he demonstrated each word, caressing and kissing and nibbling. "Tipped with nipples so glorious, I could worship them for days."

Slowly, he lowered himself to kneel before me, his lips never leaving my breasts. Hands caressing my sides, he kept talking even as our breathing sped up and my heart raced.

"Your beautiful, sexy, athletic legs. Your full firm and round ass, crying out for a caress or a spanking."

I tried to object to that, but the only noise I could make was a whimper. Looking up at me, Gragash grinned.

"And then, my beautiful, there is your pussy."

As he spoke, he slid a finger between thighs, teasing my lips with a delicate control that felt out of place on such a musclebound man. "Your amazing, wet, wanton pussy."

I whimpered something wordless and tried to speak. Failed, because Gragash slipped a finger into my channel at just the right moment to turn speech into helpless, eager mewling. With gentle, irresistible strength, he guided me down onto the blankets, spread my legs, and met my gaze.

"Your delicious pussy."

And then he dove in.

His long, dark tongue pressed between my folds, licked with eager intensity, slipped around my clit and driving me wild in an instant. I bucked under him, grabbing the blankets with both hands and pulling wildly. Gragash rumbled his appreciation, eating me out with skill and enthusiasm, enjoying every taste just as I enjoyed every stroke of his tongue.

He pushed a second finger into me, then a third. I bucked in a crazed frenzy and screamed at the heavens as his inhuman tongue lapped my clit faster and faster and *would not stop.*

The orgasm crashed over me like a wave, and I clung to Gragash as though I was drowning and he was a life raft. I don't know how long that gasping rush of ecstasy lasted—it seemed like every time I was about to recover, Gragash found some way to push me further from the shores of sanity.

Eventually, he relented. Or I passed out. Hard to tell which. When I came back to myself, I was a trembling wreck in his lap. I'd never been so sated, so drained, so happy.

He stroked my hair, watched my eyes, and looked happy, relaxed, and satisfied.

"There, little one," he whispered. "I'll hear no more about how you are 'not pretty enough.' Any vice den would be happy to have someone of your qualifications aboard, and if someone disagrees, I will teach them their error."

All I managed was a nod and a murmured agreement. Then my consciousness faded and the darkness claimed me again.

11

GRAGASH

*D*ays passed quickly and I got very little rest. Either training or attending to my human mate would have filled my time. Both together?

It kept me too busy to worry, at least.

Abigail wasn't so lucky, having nothing to prepare for, so I did my best to keep her too worn out and happy to think. Not that fucking her into a blissful daze at every opportunity was a hardship, in the least.

Lachrin station, when we reached it, was a gem-studded circle hanging over the blue backdrop of a water planet. Each gem was a habitat, I realized as the details became clear, each stunning in its own way. There, a palace of crystal; a sphere of liquid, great shapes swimming in its depths; a single, giant tree, large enough to hold a city. Glorious and beautiful, it grew in the viewport as we closed and I could have watched it for hours and never run out of fantastic sights to gawp at. Nothing in the galaxy could compare to this sight, I felt sure.

Abigail rested her hand on my forearm, squeezing and reminding me of one view I preferred. "Be careful on there, okay? No one within a light year of here gives a damn about fair play."

I turned to look at her, chuckling. "Apart from you?"

"No." The flat, angry certainty surprised her as much as me, and it took her a moment to continue. "No, Gragash. Fuck fair—all I care about is you coming out on top."

It took an effort not to roar with laughter at that, though I knew she wouldn't appreciate the humor.

"Then take comfort in this: I never fight fair. There are no rules in the arena."

Her shoulders sagged, and she took a deep breath. "Gragash, you're an amazing fighter and I've never met anyone as brave. I care about you so much. But your naïveté is going to kill me! It's not the fighting in the arena I'm worried about, it's the politics outside of it. There are people out there who'll make a fortune on this fight, and if they can manipulate the result, they will. Be careful, alright?"

I nodded agreement, though I hoped she was wrong. I'd rather face foes head-on than in some scheming game of politics. Which, when I thought about it, backed up my mate's point.

A deep booming gong drew our attention back to the present. The *Darha's Blessing* had arrived.

When Ty'anii led me down the ramp and onto the station, the difference between the view we'd had from space and what we disembarked to was overwhelming. No crystal spires or micro-gravity gardens here, just a worn and warped platform and rust-pitted machinery. The airmakers wheezed and vibrated, pushed to their limits, and yet the air was low in oxygen and tasted of burned oil and dead meat. I snarled at the unexpected, unpleasant smells, wondering how it was possible that this place, this haven of luxury for the rich, was so poorly maintained.

My Prytheen warder stumbled over a loose tile, and that was when I realized how little light there was. Plenty for an Orc, but when even a Prytheen couldn't see what she was walking on I knew it had to be bad.

"Fucking rich assholes," Fenx muttered behind me, and the rest of the crew sniggered.

"They didn't get rich spending money on their employees," Captain Vaher said with a chuckle and slapped Fenx on the back. "Every cent saved in lighting down here is one more to put into the 'Rich Assholes' Drinking Fund' so what do you think they'll do?"

Is that envy I hear? Vaher didn't have a moral objection, I was sure. He just lived close enough to his employees to get stabbed if he tried to run things this way. The kind of people who'd force their workers to labor in the dark would own a fleet of ships, not captain one of them.

The best sources of light were the other ships moored beside the *Blessing,* so the illumination was inconstant and shifting. Workers scurried around, unloading and refueling and doing all the esoteric things a space port needed done. We skirted around them and to a massive door, above which hung a sign.

Fighter's Pit
Death is Inevitable. Glory is Eternal.

Cheerful sentiments, I thought. What use is glory to a dead man? Even alive, it had never done me much good.

"Miss Ty'anii, yes?" The voice drew my attention down to a small male who looked more like a burrowing rodent than a person. His whiskers twitched as he peered through goggles. "I am Qubbins, and I have been expecting you. Some time ago, in fact"

"Mr. Qubbins!" I'd never heard her direct so much joyful enthusiasm at anyone aside from Vaher, and I couldn't tell if she was sincere. "Such a delight to finally meet you. Let me introduce our champion, Gragash."

I growled at the little creature, whose goggles whirred and whined as they focused on me.

"Dear me, he *is* a big one." Qubbins was unfazed by my looming presence, a rare trait in a slaver from my experience. Even Vaher and his crew kept their distance, but Qubbins stepped closer for a better look. I wondered what he saw through those lenses of his. "I've seen Orcs come and go, who in this business hasn't? Gragash, though, you look special."

"Should place a bet on him," Ty'anii said. "I've never regretted it."

"A bet?" The rodent-man managed to look scandalized just by the twitching of his whiskers. An impressive feat, I had to admit. "On the games I organize? Why, I've never been so insulted."

Ty'anii blinked and paled, taking a step back and opening her mouth without finding words to speak. Despite the rage burning in me, or perhaps because of it, I found that incredibly amusing. Qubbins let her hang there for a count of three before continuing.

"No, no, the bookies pay me for the privilege of operating here. Winning their money as well? I don't want to beggar them, not when they're paying good bribes."

His chittering laugh was high pitched, and the Prytheen joined in a beat too late to sound sincere. That just made Qubbins laugh harder, though.

"Now, if you'll follow me, Gragash, you'll need to hurry to get ready. I *had* a room prepared for you, but there's no time for you to rest now. Just make sure to give the quality a good show, and I'll give you the tour afterward."

That is the last thing I want to do, I thought. *Let your damned quality fight each other if they're so keen on violence.*

*I'll fight, but not for them. I'll fight for **her.***

12

ABIGAIL

*S*eparation from Gragash hurt, and the pain filled me with guilt. *I'm not with him? Tough shit. He's being thrown into a fight to the death. That's probably a bigger problem, right?*

Did thinking that help with the pain? It did not. But how could I miss this chance to beat myself up?

I walked in a daze, paying no attention to where Vaher and his gang led me. I only noticed things had changed when I stepped through a doorway and a cool breeze cut through the stifling heat. At some point, we'd left the darkness and the bare, pitted metal of the service docks behind. The room we entered now was infinitely more comfortable. My feet sank into a soft, deep carpet, a red so dark it was almost black. A subtle pattern wove through it, silver thread only visible because of the bright lighting. The seal of the Guild.

Three of the walls were black marble. The fourth was mostly occupied by a silvery shimmer, flanked by hologram sculptures of gladiators. Faint cheers carried through the forcefield—another fight? If so, I was glad I couldn't see.

Decadently comfortable furniture faced the shimmer. Chairs worth more than my apartment on Earth waited beside tables holding various refreshments. Delicate scents wafted from the dishes to make my mouth water, though after a few days on maker-mush, anything that promised actual flavor would do that.

On a planet, this room would be an impressive display of wealth.

On a space station? Obscene. Importing this weight of stone, dragging it across space, just to line a room? The only purpose was to show off the wealth and power of the owners, the same wealth they hoarded by leaving their workers in the dark. In short, exactly what I expected from Lachrin Station.

The crew of *Darha's Blessing* did their best not to show how impressed they were. Only Vaher did a reasonable job. The rest clustered near the door as though afraid they'd have to pay for anything they touched.

"Where's the quality?" one of them whispered. My laugh escaped before I could stop it. Everyone wheeled and glared, but I'd had enough of shying away from them now. I glared right back.

"What, did you think you were going to mingle with interstellar royalty? That a Guildfather would drink with you? You're getting to walk on their carpets and breathe their air. To these fucks, that's honor enough for the likes of you."

Ty'anii's snarl showed her teeth, but it was Brish who spoke. "Careful, human. Your Orc isn't here to protect you."

Fuck it. Time to call some bluffs. "He doesn't have to be. Captain Vaher knows what'll happen if any of you hurt me."

The Akedian lunged for me, but Ty'anii was quicker. She caught his wrist, twisting and slamming him into the wall with a heavy thud. Keeping him pinned there, arm twisted behind his back, she snarled at him.

"Idiot! Hurt her, and Gragash is done fighting for us. Kill her, and all he'll ever think about is how to kill us as painfully as possible."

"Yeah, well, if the *slave* goes berserk, we put him down," Brish replied. "Fucker's getting too big for his boots, anyway."

Vaher shook his head. "Brish, if you put me in a position where I have to kill the Orc, I'll feed you to him first. That fucker made us ten times more than you have, and he got us in here. Make me choose between you and him. I fucking dare you."

Brish audibly ground his teeth, then relaxed in Ty'anii's grip. His eyes locked onto me, though, and I saw that his rage and hate were strong as ever. Stronger, maybe, since I'd embarrassed him in front of his 'friends.'

I smiled at him. No point not leaning into it at this

point, right? He'd kill me if he got the chance, might as well make him miserable until then.

"If I might suggest taking your seats, the fight is about to begin." The voice from all around, speaking with a beautifully musical accent. Ty'anii grinned and gave Brish's arm a last twist before turning her back on him and sliding into the chair beside Captain Vaher. The two seats shifted and merged into a couch seamlessly. I upped my already high estimate of the furniture's value and sat as far from Brish as I could manage.

The silver shimmer vanished with a flourish, and we looked out into an arena. Golden sand gleamed under bright sunlight, and the blue planet hung huge in the sky above. Under other circumstances, it would have been a sight of breath-taking beauty. Now, all of that was a distraction, as was the audience.

There were no stands here, no cheap seats, only boxes like ours, full of people shouting and cheering. So many voices speaking at once that it sounded like noise, not words. Not that I cared what anyone was saying. My attention was focused on a platform rising from a hatch in the arena's floor.

Gragash stood there, magnificent and beautiful and smoldering with a rage that, by rights, ought to have burned the entire audience alive. He wore only a leather kilt, an armored gorget, and a gauntlet crackling with energy.

He turned, unerringly bringing his burning gaze up to mine. As though he knew exactly where to find me, as though he felt my gaze on him. As impossible as that was, it felt right and natural. Equally impossible was the calm that settled over us as we exchanged looks for what might be the last time.

Another platform ascended, and Gragash broke eye contact with me to face his opponent. I looked too, and didn't like what I saw. The newcomer was the size of Gragash, slate-gray skin covered in scales and scars, but with an extra pair of arms. Each of his four hands held a different weapon, and he looked like he knew how to use them. On his left he whirled a short, barbed spear, while holding a shield close to his body. On his right, an ax and a net. It seemed an unfair setup, and the crowd loved it.

Around me, the slavers leaned in to watch and my heart hammered loud and fast. The gray-skinned alien, Eater-of-Chains, was announced with a long list of prior victories, enough to make me worry. Surely even Gragash didn't have *that* many wins.

Fenx giggled to himself as the announcer began Gragash's intro.

"Dont'cha worry, girl," he said, voice low enough no one else would hear. "Big guy's a brute, but your Orc's got 'im."

He must have seen the confusion on my face, because he giggled again. "No point in you being scared and all, girl. Doesn't make me any richer, and talk doesn't cost me anything."

With that, he turned back to the arena, leaving me to shake my head. *I guess it's technically better to be a* *slaver who's **not** a sadist, but does he really think it makes a difference?*

I looked down at the four-armed brute squaring off against Gragash, wondering if his mate was being told the same comforting lies. It wasn't a helpful thought, and I tried to put it out of my mind as the two warriors faced off.

A bell chimed, and they leaped at each other, too fast for me to follow. Weapons flashed in the hot sun's light, and then they were past each other, spinning to assess the damage they'd dealt.

Overhead, holograms helpfully replayed the exchange of blows in slow motion. Gragash ducked under the ax, but the spear gouged down his back as he lunged. His punch struck Eater-of-Chains on the shield with a flash of light. While the shield took most of the blow, that arm didn't seem to move right afterward.

But the gash on Gragash's back was more worrying. Deep and long, blood dripped from it and my heart froze as I saw my orc lover wince. It was well-disguised, perhaps invisible to anyone else, but Gragash's injury slowed him.

Eater charged in again, attacking with speed and fury, and drove Gragash back. The orc parried and dodged, unable to land a blow in return. The spear and ax together were too fast.

The tension around me rose fast, and the slavers sat forward in their seats. I wondered what their plan was if their champion lost this fight. How much had they bet on Gragash? If they bankrupted themselves in this match, it might make Gragash's ghost happy. It wouldn't make up for the pain of losing him, but it would give me some satisfaction, too.

I winced and looked away as Eater's ax tore through Gragash's left arm, his counterpunch trapped in the net. Someone cursed and Ty'anii slammed her fist into the wall beside her, leaving a dent.

It was impossible to watch. Even more impossible to look away, to not see what happened to my beloved. Praying I wasn't going to watch him die, I uncovered my eyes and looked out over the arena sands. Gragash still stood, bloody and weakened, but for how long?

His opponent had taken his own share of injuries, but not nearly so many as my orc, and now the long reach of his spear let him keep his distance. Eater circled Gragash, watching for an opening, and Gragash turned with him, guard up.

It couldn't last. Impatient shouts from the crowd told me it had gone on too long already. Gragash dropped his guard for just a moment, and Eater lunged in, spear sliding through Gragash's belly.

I howled in pain, drowned out by the frenzied cheers from the crowd. We all fell silent as Gragash *launched himself up the spear.* His wound should have stopped him, the agony of a gut wound or the loss of blood, but he ignored those petty details, charging with a roar.

Eater-of-Chains looked as shocked as the rest of us, but he could afford the moment of frozen paralysis. Gragash's gauntleted fist slammed into Eater's throat with a crack like thunder and sent him tumbling to the sands. Clutching at his throat, he tried to get up, but Gragash hit him again.

This time he stayed down, lying still. Gragash stood over him, raising his bloody fist, and a hologram of him appeared overhead. The arena's speakers amplified his voice into a thunderous boom as lightning arced around his gauntlet.

"I dedicate this victory to Abigail ko'Gragash," he said, and his voice echoed through the arena. Then he toppled backward, slowly and majestically, to lie unmoving on the ground.

13

GRAGASH

I woke in the warm embrace of my mate, my wounds aching and sore, my head pounding with pain. Despite the pain, I wouldn't have traded it for anything, except that Abigail was crying as she lay curled up against me.

"I am alive," I told her, though the roughness of my voice made my claim sound dubious.

Abigail took it better, though, sitting up and looking at me with red eyes. Her expression hardened. "Good, because I'm going to *kill you myself*. Don't you ever put me through that again."

To emphasize her point, she thumped my chest, sending me into a coughing fit. My lungs weren't handling the injuries I'd taken well. "Oof. You don't need to demonstrate, beloved. I know you have a killer's heart."

Eyes going wide, my mate tried to leave the bed, but I caught her and dragged her back to me. The impact hurt worse than her punch had, but I this time I was prepared and hid the pain. She squirmed in my grip, though careful now not to aggravate my injuries. "Let go, idiot, I need to get the doctor."

"No, you need to stay here. You are better than any medicine, beloved mate, especially what I'd get from these monsters."

Though I resented the need to take my eyes off her, I looked beyond my mate. High-tech medical equipment hummed softly in the background, under quiet, soothing music. Bright light gleamed off the pristine white surfaces. In every way an improvement on cramped and filthy sick bay aboard the *Darha's Blessing*. A single-person room, too, though the imposing metal door with no mechanism on the inside made it clear it wasn't for my benefit.

A luxurious prison might be better than a harsh one, but it was still a prison.

Despite that, it gave me some much-needed privacy after living in a cage for years. Abigail yelped as I pulled her closer, raising my head to kiss her passionately. A moment later, I fell back to the mattress and gasped for breath. This time, Abigail took care to avoid my injuries when she hit me. I growled a mock warning, so she hit me again.

"Don't you growl at me, you were asking for that. You need to rest!"

Her eyes sparkled, but I didn't think it was just a joke. Genuine worry put a tremble in her voice, so I relented and raised my hands. "I do not wish to upset you, darling. But your kisses are all the medicine I need."

She snorted and blew a stray strand of hair out of her face. "Sure. That and the cocktail of medical nanites they pushed into you."

"Those high-tech toys are nothing compared to the power of your lips," I said with every bit of sincerity I could manage. I was at least half-serious: Abigail's touch felt better than any medicine I'd ever had. When she wasn't punching me, anyway.

"Oh?" The sparkle in my mate's eyes intensified as a wicked grin appeared on her lips. "In that case, let me put my powers to good use."

I answered her grin with my own and reached for her, only to have my hand swatted away. "Nope. You need to rest. Stay still."

Curious, I let my hand fall back to the mattress, and Abigail leaned in to plant a kiss on the side of my neck. A scorching inferno ignited my nervous system, pure joy radiating from each touch of her lips.

"No." Her voice was as firm as her hand as she caught my wrist and pushed it back down. I hadn't even realized I'd lifted it.

She kept kissing me, working down to the hollow of my throat, then across and along my mending collarbone. Every time I moved, or tried to, she pushed me back into the mattress. I didn't resist, lying back and enjoying every soft kiss, every little bite.

Slow and steady, she kissed her way down my body, touching on every injury, every scar. She pulled back the sheet as she went, revealing my body a little at a time, teasing us both. An eternity of agonizing anticipation later, her lips finally reached my waist, igniting a surge of desire in me. We both breathed heavily and my fingers dug into the bed to keep me from grabbing her.

It took all my self-discipline, and even then it was a close-run thing. The urge to take her, to hold her, to claim her as *mine*, was almost too much. Abigail didn't make it easier with her little gasp of awe as she flipped back the sheet and uncovered my erection.

Her warm breath caressed my skin, and my cock trembled under it. Her giggle was part nerves, part excitement, and by the Old Gods it made me harden even further. After a moment's hesitation, she ran a finger down my shaft, tracing the veins.

I drew breath to speak, only for Abigail to lay a finger of her free hand over my lips, shushing me. Instead, I sucked her finger into my mouth, my tongue circling it, winning a tiny shiver of delight from her.

She moaned and slipped her lips around me, her warm tongue lapping at the head of my cock and making me shudder and reach for her again. My mate pulled her finger free of my mouth and wagged it at me, the message clear: *don't you **dare** exert yourself.* And while I felt tempted to see what she'd do to enforce the rule, I did my best to give her what she wanted. To stay still, control my responses, and enjoy the gift she gave me.

"Fuck," I groaned, my mate's dexterous tongue

teasing my cock head until arched my back and sweat beaded on my forehead. "Fucking *fuck.*"

Her chuckle at my vocabulary vibrated through me, my cock pulsing in her mouth, and holding back my orgasm was as daunting a task as I could imagine. My nails clawed at the sheets, bit into the smartmaterial mattress beneath. My back arched, but I kept my control. Fought for it, kept it.

Then she gripped my shaft in her hands, stroking and kissing and sucking, and I lost it. With a roar, I grabbed Abigail, smartmaterial trailing from my fingers in foamy strips. She squeaked, squirmed, and struggled helplessly as I lifted her. With a rough laugh, I turned and flung her onto the bed. Though my bruised and battered body ached, it couldn't dissuade me. My heart ached for her and my soul blazed like a supernova against the darkness.

I would not be denied.

Her clothes came apart under my hands, fabric shredding and scattering. In moments, only scraps remained, doing nothing to hide her body from my hungry gaze. There was no finer sight in all the galaxy than my mate's beautiful curves, glistening skin, her breasts rising and falling quickly as she panted for air. Cheeks bright red, eyes wide, lips curled into a wild grin that would tempt a monk.

"I wondered how long it would take for—*eek!*"

She'd silenced me with the touch of a finger. I was less gentle, grabbing her knees and pulling her to me. My cock rubbed across her pussy, feeling the wet folds part for me. There were no words in my mind, nothing but the act of taking and claiming my mate all over again.

She reached between us as I kissed and bit my way across her neck and shoulders, my throbbing cock pressed to the welcoming wet warmth between her legs. Urgent and demanding, she pulled me to her, and my thrust met her with a brutal force that drove her into the remains of the mattress.

Abigail bucked under me as she cried out and pulled me closer, her legs wrapping around my waist while her hands pulled me in. I didn't need the urging. With each thrust, I drove deeper into her and her cries of pleasure filled the room.

Already on edge from Abigail's teasing, my orgasm built fast. When her inner walls clamped down on me, I knew she was there as well. Our bodies joined in a feedback loop that lifted us higher, far into the storm clouds of our shared ecstasy.

I struggled to regain control, refusing to come before my beloved partner. Every thrust into her tight, wet sex made it harder to fight my body's needs. Every thrust, she gripped tighter, fitting me perfectly, and my cock thrummed with need, sending her wild. She writhed, crying out my name, and I could resist no longer. With a roar of triumph, I exploded inside her, and we fell together onto the tattered remnants of the medical bed, clinging to each other for support.

14

ABIGAIL

Gragash was alive. I clung to that thought as much as I clung to him, feeling his chest rise and fall, his heart beat loud and slow and steady now. It looked like we'd gotten through the fight, but this had just been the introduction. The true fight was still to come, and looking at my sleeping Orc hero, I knew two things.

First, that he would fight any foe to keep me safe.

Second, that Captain Vaher would push him into worse and worse fights until one killed him.

Unacceptable. There has to be another way. I tried to think, which was difficult when I was looking at the worst outcome possible. Running was out of the question—I doubted we'd even get past the door. Despite the high-tech healing equipment, the room was more like a cell than a medical facility. Even if we escaped, where would we go? We had no friends aboard Lachrin, no allies aside from the Orcs in the hold of the

Blessing. Which was another problem. Gragash wasn't about to abandon his kin, but rescuing them would be the most predictable move in the universe. We'd be walking into a trap.

Gragash lay still, only his heartbeat and the slow rise and fall of his chest letting me know he was still among the living. I let him rest, knowing I'd disrupted his healing too much already. There was no point in waking him up and worrying him.

I was no closer to an answer when the door's lock disengaged with a loud *clunk* and it slid open. Beneath my head, Gragash's heart sped up a little, but he gave no sign of waking.

A doctor strode into the room, tall and spindly, with skin cracked like bark. He looked like an old tree on which someone had hung a lab coat. I thought he was the same doctor who treated Gragash's wounds, but I couldn't be sure. He seemed cheerful until he looked up from his tablet and saw the state of the room.

"Ten Thousand Suns, what have you *done?*"

I looked at the medical bed, its smartmaterial mattress gutted, the covers ripped apart and discarded. Screens showed various alerts, though apparently none serious enough to call someone to help. My cheeks warmed as he stared at us, at the bed, back at us.

He threw up his hands and sighed. "This is how you repay me for fixing him? For letting you in to visit him? I expected you to fuck him, not murder my equipment!"

"Sorry, sorry." I did my best to be disarming and charming, but the doctor seemed impervious. I guess that made sense for a doctor hired to tend gladiator-slaves' injuries—having empathy for his patients would make his job a soul-crushing nightmare.

I blinked. *He had enough sympathy to let me visit Gragash. He didn't even try for a bribe, not that I have anything to offer.* There had to be a reason, perhaps something I could lean on. We needed help, even if was from a slave-doctor.

Trying to think of him as a source for a story rather than an accomplice to slavery, I gave him a sheepish smile. "Gragash got carried away, Doctor, I'm really sorry. I'm sure his owners will pay for repairs, though."

"They'd better." I recognized that tone—the Akedian grumbled because he liked to, but unless I missed my guess, he was looking forward to telling this story. That was a motivation I understood.

Better, it was a motivation I knew how to exploit.

"You must get the most fascinating clients coming through your surgery, Doctor," I said with a wide-eyed, innocent smile, keying my implants to record.

"...AND what I thought was a parasite was actually their king!" Doctor Zsisk finished with a laugh. "Which is how I came to need another job in a hurry, and couldn't be too picky."

I smiled, and nodded, and sipped the weirdly textured water he called 'tea.'

"You should write a book someday. You've got some great stories."

I wasn't lying, not really. The doctor might not be as good a storyteller as he thought he was, and his stories were trite, but I'd read worse books. He'd probably make money on a tell-all autobiography, assuming his former clients didn't kill him first.

He warmed to me quickly once I started listening to his stories, and even gave me a tunic to wear, replacing the clothes Gragash had torn from me so delightfully. It was a simple, disposable thing, maker-printed and unflattering, but at least I wasn't naked when Vaher and Ty'anii came to check on their investment.

The quick back-and-forth between Ziska and Vaher was incomprehensible to me, but Vaher seemed happy enough and passed across a credit chip. I took that as good news for Gragash—the doctor had assured me he'd make a full recovery, but I didn't know if he was the type to lie to avoid a scene. Lying to his paying customer was a lot less likely.

Ty'anii grabbed me by the scruff of the neck, giving me no choice but to go with them when they left. I tried to protest, then fell silent as her claws pricked my skin.

"What a fucking shitshow," Vaher said. As soon as the door closed behind us, a scowl replaced his friendly smile. "That was supposed to be an easy fight. Just a warmup, they said. Something to give the locals a taste of Gragash. Instead, I'm paying over the odds for a lung replacement and muscle repair and... whatever a 'pynloss procedure' is. Probably medical jargon for 'soak the customer for all he's got.'"

He stalked ahead through the arena's slave hospital. Dozens of small rooms like Gragash's opened off the broad, sterile corridor. Most were open and unoccupied, and I saw no sign of anyone else. Was it this empty when I arrived? I couldn't remember—Gragash's wounds had my full attention then.

"Too quiet," Ty'anii said, echoing my fears. "Where is everyone? Place was busy when we came in."

Vaher paused and looked around, lips tightening. "Fuck."

He drew a pair of small pistols from under his coat, tossing one to Ty'anii. As though that was a signal, a Drall stepped out into the corridor ahead of us.

Ty'anii hissed and stepped in front of her captain. I doubted it would help him. The newcomer stood as tall as Gragash, but Drall walk on all fours. He was a massive, all muscle and leathery hide, with a mouth big enough to bite someone's head off and small eyes that glimmered with malice. The formal robe he wore looked out of place on his massive bulk, but it identified him as a Guild member.

I braced myself to run. If this was an ambush, I wouldn't bet on Vaher coming out on top, and I certainly didn't want to be standing anywhere near him when the fight started.

The Drall smirked. "Don't worry yourselves. Boss wants a word, that's all."

With that, he stepped aside, leaving space for us to enter the room he'd emerged from. I considered running anyway, but there was nowhere to hide, so I squeezed past the menacing Drall and into another medical cell.

It was crowded inside, though the bed had been removed to make room for a pair of comfortable chairs. One was empty, and on the other sat a small Vehn male in a deep purple robe, silvery stitching marking the Guild's symbol on it. He looked old, with a weathered face and gray feathers in place of hair, but his smile was warm and his eyes clear. A pair of Prytheen warriors flanked him, adding an air of menace. Without them, he'd have looked like a kindly grandfather.

I didn't let it fool me. He wore the robes of a Guildfather, and no one gets that high in the Guild of Criminals by being nice.

"Captain Vaher," the little old man said, voice warm and strong despite his years. "Qubbins speaks highly of you and your crew, and I value his judgement. Come, have a seat. I have an offer for you."

An offer he can't refuse, I thought. Vaher and Ty'anii exchanged a look showing they'd had the same thought. Vaher took the offered seat and returned the old Guildfather's smile.

"What can we do for you, sir?"

"I trust this will stay between us?" he waited for Vaher's enthusiastic nod before continuing. "You've brought some excitement to the arena. New blood, fresh face, and a dramatic win. A classic story. The thing is, he's a little more than I expected. Qubbins gives your fighter even odds against my good friend Korsar."

He nodded at the doorway, and the Drall outside rumbled something in acknowledgement. *That* was who Gragash was supposed to fight? I shuddered at the thought.

"Commitments have been made," Vaher said, tone light. "It would be difficult to back out of the fight now."

"Indeed. Indeed. But that's not what I had in mind, no. I'd just like things to run according to plan."

A pause that seemed to stretch out into infinity followed, then Vaher said carefully. "Your original plan called for Gragash to die in the arena. I've made a considerable investment in that orc."

"I appreciate that. We're only having this conversation because you might make a valuable partner, and I don't want to start off on the wrong foot." The old Vehn ran a hand over his feathered scalp and chuckled. "I can't just bury your crew in gold. This has to be discrete. The audience at large wouldn't appreciate the subtleties involved, and might take offense. Still, I have heard the *Darha's Blessing* has a hold full of slaves? A friend of mine will pay over the odds for them as arena fodder."

My blood ran cold at that, remembering the orc children I'd seen aboard the *Blessing.* They'd be thrown into the arena to die? It didn't bear thinking about. *Even Vaher can't go for this,* I tried to tell myself.

It was nonsense, of course. The slaver captain sailed straight past any moral quandries to start haggling over price. "That would have to be quite generous indeed to make up for the lost income."

One of the Guildfather's bodyguards pulled out a contract and showed it to Vaher. The other opened a case to display the Credits Imperial inside, a glittering array of coins. I couldn't see the amount, but Vaher pulled a pen from his coat with a decisiveness that told me all I needed to know.

Whatever the Guildfather offered, it was more than enough.

15

GRAGASH

My second awakening was a lot less pleasant than my first. There was an empty chill where my mate had lain, and instead, Captain Vaher leaned against the shining white wall, again engrossed in his holographic reports.

We were alone. Even if Ty'anii was right outside the door, she couldn't react fast enough if I attacked now. Tensing and untensing my muscles told me the nanites had done their work—none of my injuries would get in my way.

It was a pleasant fantasy, but nothing more. I couldn't kill this man until I'd somehow saved my kin and my mate.

"What do you want, Vaher? You're the last person I want to wake up to." Usually, I'd be more polite. After the fight I'd won and the money I'd made him, I figured the captain could deal with a bit of honesty.

It seemed I was right. Vaher swept his holograms

away with a gesture and smiled his least-fake smile. "Ah, Gragash, old friend. I'm glad to see your spirits are high. You've done spectacularly."

"Good. Now fuck off and let me rest."

"Now, there are things we need to discuss first." Vaher stepped away from the wall, rubbing his palms together, and I waited stoically until he continued. "This is going to be a hard ask, old friend, but I need a favor from you. I need you to throw the fight with Korsar."

That startled a snorted laugh out of me, followed by a groan. My ribs weren't fully healed yet. "Are you going into comedy, Vaher? Giving up the piracy and going straight as an entertainer is a bold course, but I'd support you."

He just looked at me, one eyebrow raised, waiting until I continued. "I know that is a joke, because we're talking about a *fight to the death*. My honor would not permit me to throw any fight, but nobody would be stupid enough to die just so that you can clean up in some shady scam."

Vaher said nothing, which wasn't like him. I folded my arms and met silence with silence, sure that I could out-stubborn him. It didn't take long.

"Fine," he said, throwing his hands up in disgust. "This isn't about money, it's about us all not being murdered by Guild assassins. And by all, I include your precious Abigail and your kin. The fucking local Guildfather wants his pet fighter to win, so that's how it's got to be."

It wasn't funny, but I laughed anyway. My only other choice was to tear the hypocrite's head off, and that wouldn't help. "You're mad because someone else is rigging the matches, and you don't like to lose. Fuck that, we are not on the same side here. And if you're claiming you won't profit from this, you're insulting my intelligence."

"Yes, fine. I'm going to bet against you through a cutout, so I'll make a lot off this if you lose. Win and you'd ruin me, but the price would be everyone aboard *Darha's Blessing*."

I shrugged. "They'd move from being your slaves to being someone else's. I don't like that idea, but it's not that big a change, and I'd be alive to see them."

Vaher ground his teeth, then stopped as he realized what he was doing. "This a problem for both of us, and we can only face it together. I know this is a lot to ask, but I'll make sacrifices too. Your kin—I'll free them, give them each enough money to get by, and let them off at any nearby world they want."

My eyes narrowed, trying to judge the crimson-skinned slaver. There wasn't much point. I didn't trust him, and there wasn't anything he could do or say to change that. His fear seemed genuine, though, and that was the lynchpin of this proposal. Maybe he was being honest.

If not, there wasn't much I could do about it. Glaring at my captor, I nodded reluctantly. Even a chance of freeing Abigail and the rest of my family was worth sacrificing for.

She would disagree. I sighed. Saying goodbye would not be easy, and I expected to get punched again. "How can I trust you to keep your word?"

The captain relaxed visibly at my agreement. "I have a contract ready for our signatures and enforceable under Guild rules. Thank you for being reasonable, Gragash."

At his gesture, one of the hologram documents reappeared, and he turned it for me to see. It seemed to say what I needed it to, without specifying what services I provided in exchange. Would it bind him? I had no idea. It wasn't as though I had a lawyer to consult.

"Send my copy to Abigail," I said, pressing my thumb into the page to mark my agreement. "She's the one who'll need it."

16

ABIGAIL

Ty'anii didn't tell me where she was taking me. As soon as we'd left the Guildfather and his goons behind, she grabbed me by the scruff of the neck as though I was an unruly kitten, and dragged me away.

It didn't take me long to realize we were heading back to the *Blessing,* though, and I understood. I'd heard the entire deal, and if I told Gragash what they planned to do with his family there was no chance he'd go along with it. They had to keep us apart.

So when she threw me into the hold and a dozen pairs of orcish eyes stared at me, it didn't come as a shock. Of course they'd keep all their hostages together. Easier that way. That didn't make it any less intimidating to look up at them. Even the kids looked like they could take me in a fight, and the adults…

"Who the fuck are you, urd'ash?"

The female who spoke loomed over me, anger

flaring in her dark eyes, muscles taut under green skin. The family resemblance was undeniable, I saw Gragash in her face and her shoulders and her anger.

"Jarchess, right?" I tried to get up. A firm hand gripped my neck and pushed me back down. She looked less angry but more suspicious, and no less dangerous to me. "You're Gragash's sister?"

"I know who I am," she snarled. "I asked who you are, urd'ash."

Sharp claws pricked my skin, and I swallowed nervously. In Gragash's hands, I'd always felt safe. His sister was a different story.

"I'm Abigail," I started, then paused. *Crap, how did he say it?* "Abigail ko'Gragash. Your brother needs our help."

Apparently I said it right, because Jarchess let go of my throat and stepped back, giving me space to rise. Her eyes raked me up and down, and I wasn't sure if her expression was a smile or a sneer. "Yes, I can see Gragash picking you. Welcome to the clan. By tradition, I should offer to share wine with you, but all our captors leave us with is funny-tasting water. Want some?"

Not about to reject an orc custom, I nodded eagerly and took the offered flask. The water was warm, had a metallic tang, and at the same time it tasted like *hope*.

"We don't have long," I said, wiping mouth and passing the flask back. "Gragash is in trouble, and so are we."

17

GRAGASH

My requests to see Abigail before the fight went unacknowledged. When I escalated them to demands, Vaher sighed and told me he'd see what he could do. There were, he said, bigger issues at play.

And now a motorized platform lifted me into the sunlight again, without me having a chance to say goodbye to my mate. It was enough to make me consider not cooperating with the slaver's plan, but that would just be a disaster for Abigail and the others.

So, snarling and frustrated, I stepped back out onto the arena sands. A roar of approval greeted me, people chanting my name. I gave it no attention, turning instead to the owners' box to look for my mate.

Sure enough, there she was, at Captain Vaher's side. He lounged comfortably in his chair, utterly at ease with the world. But Abigail? I'd expected grief or anger if she knew the plan, hope if she did not. Instead, her eyes were full of determination, a hardness I'd not known she had in her.

A shame I would never get to appreciate it close up. Behind me, the second hatch opened, a platform rising slowly, bearing a Drall warrior into view. He was huge, muscular even by that species' standards, and even on all fours, he stood as tall as me. Korsar.

The Guild champion wore little more than a leather harness, showing off intricate Guild tattoos. No weapons, but his claws and teeth were weapon enough. He stepped off the platform, he moved with a grace I'd only seen on the most skilled of fighters.

*The Guildfather was worried I'd beat **this**?* I snorted and shook my head. *Could have saved himself the trouble of fixing the fight. I'm not sure how I'd go about winning if I tried.*

The announcer was still listing victories, whether mine or my opponents I didn't care. I turned back to offer what farewells I could from this distance, catching Abigail's eye.

She shook her head, mouthing a single word clearly. **Win.**

I frowned, and she repeated herself emphatically. My frown deepened. *Does she know the danger she's in? What will happen to us all if I defeat that beast?*

Every fiber of my being cried out to trust my mate. But, if she didn't have all the facts, she couldn't know the right course to take.

What if she had information I didn't? Doubt paralyzed me, doubt and frustration. Abigail obviously shared that—even at this distance, I recognized her frustrated eye roll for what it was. As discretely as possible, she gestured to Captain Vaher.

No, past him, to a figure almost invisible in the shadows behind him. Jarchess! They'd brought her up as well. I suppose it made sense to let her watch the fight that would win her freedom, and in her place, I'd have done the same.

Except I'd plan on joining in the fight as soon as possible. My sister showed no signs of leaping into action. *Good. It would suck to fight for her freedom, only for her to die in the brawl.* But something still felt wrong. Jarchess didn't seem happy at her impending freedom, or sad at my immanent demise. She looked *angry*.

As though we were being cheated...

"The Guildfather sends his regards." Korsar's rumble pulled me out of my thoughts. Technically, it might qualify as a whisper, if one was generous or deaf. "Make it good and I promise, the end will be quick and painless. I don't mind if you get a couple of good hits in first, make the thing look real."

The consummate professional. I choked down the impulse to laugh. Here he was, talking as though I was a colleague, when he was planning on ending my life. He wouldn't be rude about it, though.

It made my decision easier, at least. The Drall, no less than the Guildfather, saw lives as mere bargaining chips. My lips curled in what my enemy probably thought was a smile, and I nodded.

"No hard feelings," I said. "If we're going to do this, let's do it as professionals."

Korsar raised a forelimb, offering it to me. Taking his hand in mine, I shook it once, hard.

I will bathe in your rancid blood, Drall. And offer your still-beating heart to my mate.

18

ABIGAIL

The bell chimed, and the two warriors charged. I set down the glass I'd been fidgeting with and tried to keep my hands shaking from being visible. Clasping them behind my back felt odd and awkward.

Holding them in front of me seemed weirdly formal. And the maker-printed dress I wore had no pockets, of course.

And if you think I was avoiding thinking about the fight going on in the arena below me, then you're damned right.

"Your orc is putting on a good show," Vaher said, popping a sliver of something blue and crunchy into his mouth. "Pity, really. He's got a lot of talent, a shame I won't be making any money off him after this."

One way or another, that's true. I didn't trust myself to say anything, so I made a noncommittal noise and hoped that would do. It was a safe bet. Vaher didn't talk to hear someone else's voice.

All around the crowd let out a gasp of surprise, and I couldn't help myself. I looked out in time to catch the slow motion hologram replay of Korsar charging, Gragash caught out by his surprising turn of speed, only to throw himself under the Drall. Lightning cracked in the dust cloud the Drall kicked up, and the monster stumbled and fell. Both rose as the dust settled, neither quite as graceful as they'd been before the clash.

I looked away from the next exchange, then peeked out to see Gragash pulling himself to his feet again. Korsar circled him, careful not to get too close. At least Gragash had frightened him. It wasn't much, but I'd take what hope I found.

Korsar charged, then dropped and skidded across the sand, taking Gragash by surprise. He got a solid punch in, but the impact sent him flying against the arena wall, and while he pulled himself to his feet, Korsar bounced up and charged again. I saw what would happen as plain as anything.

The Drall would take a hit, but he'd crush Gragash between his weight and the unyielding wall. Slowed as he was, Gragash wouldn't get out of the way in time.

I couldn't watch this. I *had to* watch it.

Only a few days ago, Vaher threw me to Gragash as a treat, expecting me to die. Now I couldn't imagine life without my orc lover, and my heart stopped as Korsar slammed into him. All around us, the crowd went wild, the rich and famous leaning out of their boxes to scream and cheer for the bloody death of an orc who was a better person than any ten of them put together. If looks could kill, I'd have scythed the arena in half with mine.

Korsar screamed too, not in triumph but in pain and frustration. I looked down and gasped—Gragash had dodged the crushing charge the only way he could. He'd gone *up,* landing on the Drall's back and riding him like a bucking stallion.

His leg was trapped between Korsar and the wall, leaving a bloody smear as the huge alien tried to shake him off. The orc hung on grimly, hands digging into the Drall's neck, and turned his face up toward me.

Agony written into every line of his expression, but his eyes showed something else. I felt the impact of his love struck my heart like a hammer, the only surrender he'd ever make. For me, those dark eyes said he'd give up everything, even his life.

But I didn't want him to die for me. I needed him to live for me. I nodded.

Korsar twisted to bite, and Gragash struck, driving his gauntleted fist into the Drall's open mouth. Lightning cracked, the big alien bucked, smoke rising from his lips as he tumbled to the sand.

Flung free by the fall, Gragash rolled and tried to get to his feet, but his crushed leg wouldn't support his weight. The arena fell silent as he rose, then fell again. But he was moving.

His opponent wasn't.

He'd won.

I vaulted out of the box, landing hard on the packed sand of the arena. Pain flashed through me, my ankle twisting on impact. I ignored that and ran for my orc.

Behind me, chaos. I glanced back to see Ty'anii, caught by surprise as much as anyone, trying to give chase. As she reached the railing, though, Jarchess hit her in a blur of green, and the two of them tumbled out of view. Vaher lurched to his feet, red face pale, scrambling for something to say or do. Anything that would ward off the Guildfather's inevitable revenge.

I wanted to laugh, to tell him I'd take care of that for him. Instead, I put my head down and ran into Gragash's powerful arms. He swept me into a kiss, not caring that hundreds, maybe thousands, were watching. Above us, a hologram bloomed, showing our embrace. My prayers were answered.

I raised my hand over my head, palm upward, and hit *play*.

"Gragash must lose. Arrange it and I'll pay you well for your trouble and discretion." The Guildfather's thin voice, instantly recognizable, boomed through the arena. The giant hologram of him forcing Vaher into fixing the fight played out overhead.

Shocked gasps from the crowd met it, followed by a deadly silence as they listened to the conversation play on. Hundreds of the wealthiest scumbags in the galaxy watched the kindly Vehn grandfather fix the fight they'd gambled on. Every face turned, slowly and steadily, towards the box reserved for the Guild of Criminals and Allied Trades.

"You fucking cheat!" I didn't see who shouted that, or who started the shooting. I didn't care, either. As though it was a signal, everyone else opened fire. Blaster bolts and laser beams criss-crossed the arena. Most targeted the Guildfather's box, others aimed for Vaher, and a few used the chaos to take shots at their rivals.

"Glorious chaos." Jarchess clapped me on the shoulder, nearly giving me a heart attack. That drew my attention back to the pressing problem of survival. "You've started a war between some of the worst people in the galaxy. Let's leave them to it."

She lifted Gragash, and I slipped under his arm to take some of his weight.

19

GRAGASH

This awakening was less pleasant than the last. Alarms blared, smoke filled the air, and everything hurt. *If this is the afterlife, the gods can keep it,* I thought.

Forcing my eyes open, I saw Abigail standing ahead of me. Her presence changed my mind—afterlife, torture pit, whatever this was, it was the best place in the galaxy because she was there.

My eyes fluttered shut again, and then *nothing*.

"—can't you fucking take your own weight?" I recognized the voice, but couldn't place it. Raising my head was too hard, even opening my eyes was a struggle.

"Give him a break," another voice shouted over the sound of blaster fire. Abigail! I relaxed—if she was here, everything was well. "He had a Drall roll over him."

"Yeah, sure, my brother will use anything as an excuse."

What is Jarchess doing here? I sank back into the darkness before I had an answer.

Cold metal under my back pulled me back out of the darkness. The familiar sounds of looting followed, my sister's grumbling along with it. *Isn't she a captive?* I tried to think straight, but it hurt too much. My head felt like it was about to explode, my leg like someone was taking a hammer to it, every part of me was sore or broken.

"They call this a medbay?" Jarchess's complaint came along with the sound of shelves being emptied onto the floor. Glass broke, metal clattered away, and Jarchess kept searching. I listened, finding it strangely soothing. Or perhaps that was the warm hand gripping mine. *Abigail,* I remembered, and smiled.

"Ah, I knew they had to have the good shit somewhere," my sister said triumphantly. "Now let's get him—"

She said more, but I heard none of it. Something ice-cold struck my injured leg, followed by a wonderful, carefree numbness.

20

ABIGAIL

At first, Gragash woke slowly, eyes flickering open. Then all at once, he sat up with a gasp, sending water sloshing everywhere. I laughed and hugged him gently.

"It's fine, beloved. You're safe. We're all safe, thanks to you."

His heart slowed and instead of searching the illusory jungle for enemies, he turned his gaze on me. As ever, the intensity made me blush and squirm. As ever, he enjoyed that, and ran his hand over my naked body.

"Then that was not a dream?" he asked carefully, like someone trying not to put too much weight on the answer. When I nodded, he relaxed visibly and held me close.

"Not a dream, my love. We're free and clear aboard the *Darha's Blessing*. You've been out of it for about a day, but the military-grade medical nanites Jarchess found have fixed up everything, even your leg."

I'd prepared the report, tried to tell him everything he needed to know as quickly as possible. One thing I hadn't prepared for was the emotional impact—tears welled in my eyes, and I choked on the words.

Gragash calmed me with a kiss. Or at least, calmed my tears. A few seconds in, it stopped being soothing and became exciting, our naked bodies pressing together in the water of the pool.

When our lips separated, my heart raced. Gragash ran his hand down my side, pressing in with his claws and making me shiver.

"Why are we in the pool?" he asked in a whisper, biting my neck when I started to answer and chuckling as my words turned into a needy groan.

I gathered myself and tried again. "More restful for your leg, more hygienic than the *Blessing's* cesspool of a medbay, and I figured you'd want to celebrate when you woke up. Besides, it gave me an excuse to snuggle you."

Wrapping my legs around him, I pulled myself close. His cock felt even harder under the water, and I moaned again, rubbing against it.

A hungry growl from Gragash only pushed me onward, and I sank my teeth into his neck. That turned his growl into a roar of passion, and he lifted me up. I squirmed as he rained kisses and bites down the front of my body. His teeth made me cry out too, the sound echoing strangely as he carried me through the water to the waterfall.

Warm water cascaded down onto us and he laid me

down on a ledge beneath the flow, soft vines cushioning the stone. He continued his loving trail of kisses down my body, spread my legs wide, and growled again.

I shuddered, reaching down to caress his face before he ducked down to lick me with his long, powerful tongue. My moans of pleasure filled the grove as my orc lover worshipped me, licking between my folds, teasing my clit, pushing me towards an orgasm, then letting me fall back.

With a whimper, I tried to draw him closer. No, no way would I move him against his will. And while he held my hips, I wasn't going to move either. He had me.

Trapped.

Pinned.

Helpless.

Exactly where I wanted to be. Because in his arms, I was safe. No matter what, I knew he wouldn't hurt me, wouldn't harm me. Tease, infuriate, frustrate? Yes, but never harm.

His tongue, dexterous and rough, sped up, and my fingers clutched his hair as he licked around my clit.

"Please," I gasped. "Please, Gragash, I need you."

He looked up at me, eyes sparkling, and redoubled his efforts. The orgasm was on me before I knew it, turning my pleading moans into wordless whimpers, and I thrashed in his arms as he held me close until I had control of myself again.

"Such an eager girl," he growled, winning a fresh blush from me. Along with an enthusiastic nod.

"I love this, love every part of this," I said. "I love you, Gragash."

"And I love you." His eyes met mine, glinting in the light. "I love all of you."

His hands demonstrated, running across my skin, squeezing my breasts and massaging them. I arched my back and moaned as his claws raked across my sensitive skin.

"I *need* you, Gragash. Please."

A pleased noise left his throat and he grinned, gripping my ass, claws biting in. He lifted me to his throbbing cock, positioned himself against me and ... stopped.

Just long enough for me to shiver with need, to look him in the eye, to plead wordlessly. And then he thrust as he pushed me down onto him. Burying his monster cock in me, forcing me to take it all in one sweet, brutal motion. A flash of delicious pain washed through me, drowned instantly by the rolling waves of pleasure.

His hungry, desperate snarl told me he felt it as much as I did, and then he moved. Rammed into me with enough force to make me scream with ecstasy on each powerful thrust. I tried to say something, to urge him on, but Gragash didn't need my encouragement. He slammed into me, pressed me back against the rocks, water flowing over us as he held nothing back.

I came again as his cock thrummed inside me, as he trapped me between his rock-hardness and the stones behind me, as he pounded me over and over. And he snarled his need, ducked his head to savage my neck, grew harder inside me. Trembled on the edge.

Carried me over it.

We came together, an explosion of joy and love and incredible pleasure that made me scream again. My pleasure and his mixed, and for a long moment we held each other, panting. Then Gragash lowered us to the rock shelf, cradling me against him.

"Wow." I smiled up at my orc lover. "Gragash, I love you, but let's never do anything that stupid again."

His laugh was warm and loving, and he kissed my forehead with gentle strength. "I am afraid I cannot make you that promise. I think we'll get into plenty of trouble together."

EPILOGUE

Undercover in the Arena. I ran my finger over the book's cover, hardly able to believe it. Bad enough that I'd written a book, but one that came out in *print?* It seemed impossible.

"Congratulations, my beloved," Gragash said, and slipped an arm around my waist to squeeze me gently. Which from him still meant tight enough to force the air from my lungs. He chuckled at my *oof* and let go.

He seemed bemused by the whole book thing, but he showed his pride in my accomplishment, even if he didn't understand it. One more thing to love about the hulking brute the universe had bound me to.

The *Orc's Nest*—no one wanted to keep the name *Darha's Blessing*—stood ready to greet us. Freshly painted, hull re-patched, it looked better than it had in years. Those repairs cost us all the operating budget, though. We needed to make a profit quickly, the orc kids ate a lot.

I grinned up at Gragash. "So, what first, *Captain* Gragash?"

He pretended to ponder the question. "First? Hm. The kosh-ra, I think. An important orcish tradition."

I still only knew a few words of orcish. That wasn't among them. "What's that me—*ah!*"

The question turned into a startled yelp as he answered by picking me up and throwing me over his shoulder. By the time we reached the ship, I was laughing and blushing.

"Jarchess is first mate. She will find us a client," he said as he bounded up the boarding ramp. "It has been far too long since we were naked together."

"We got out of bed *three hours ago,*" I protested, winning myself a playful slap on the ass.

"As I said, far too long."

My orc has his priorities, I thought to myself with a happy smile. They were priorities I'd never object to.

The End

Thank you for reading *Claimed by the Orc!* Please take a moment to leave an opinion about the book, I appreciate every review.

Check out my website or join my mailing list (Leslie Chase newsletter) for news of my upcoming releases.

And if you're on Facebook, join Leslie's Legion to connect with me and your fellow readers!

ORCS UNBOUND

Orcs Unbound is a shared world full of dominant, devoted orcs who love fiercely and forever. This series of steamy orc romances can be read in any order.

You can find them all here: Orcs Unbound

MY MONSTER, MY PROTECTOR

This series of steamy alien and monster romances can be read in any order. You can find them all here: My Monster, My Protector

- Protected by the Alien Warmachine
- Protected by the Alien King
- Protected by the Alien Bodyguard
- Protected by the Alien Mercenary
- Protected by the Alien Knight
- Protected by the Alien Space Guardian
- Protected by the Cursed Gargoyle
- Protected by the Wild Bigfoot
- Protected by the Lich Warrior

THE CRASHLAND CHRONICLES

CRASHLAND COLONY ROMANCES

Auric

Crashed on an unexplored planet, with only an alien warrior and a holographic cat for company... what's a girl to do?

Torran

Stranded on the wrong planet, captured by brutal alien raiders, the only good thing about Lisa's situation is Torran. He's a dangerous alien warrior - who also happens to be the hottest man she's ever met. Strong, protective, and lethal, he's everything she could want or need.

Perhaps she shouldn't have shot him on sight?

Ronan

Trapped with a sexy alien warrior, a holographic owl, and a mystery she needs to solve. Becca doesn't like the Prytheen, she doesn't trust them, and she is absolutely not interested in this one.

So why is she having so much trouble keeping her hands off him?

CRASHLAND CASTAWAY ROMANCES

BOUND TO THE ALIEN BARBARIAN

Crashed on the wrong planet.

Stuck with the wrong man.

Taken by the right alien.

Waking up to find she's one of only two humans to survive a crash is bad. Being captured by an alien warrior who isn't sure if she's a demon is worse. But when the alien claims her as his mate, she doesn't know if she wants to escape…

CHAINED TO THE ALIEN CHAMPION

Marakz is the hottest man I've ever seen. Also the most infuriating. At least Lord Pouncington likes him…

Diplomatic contact between the Joint Colony and the Zrin gets off to a rocky start when the Zrin champion sees his mate amongst the humans. When disaster strikes, she's his first thought — but is he rescuing her or capturing her?

Megan isn't sure she cares.

TIED TO THE ALIEN TYRANT

Tzaron says he needs me for my technical skills, but I know better.

Every smoldering glance, every touch of his skin, even the tone of his voice tells me he wants more. He wants me.

And the worst thing is, the longer I'm his prisoner, the less I want to escape.

Captured by a Zrin warlord, Victoria's first instinct is to escape. But running off into the Crashland jungle is suicide, so for now, she's stuck with the brute.

Except he's not nearly as brutish as she assumed, and the longer she's with him, the less she wants to flee from him.

CRASHLAND CONTACT ROMANCES

JOINED TO THE ALIEN SKYMASTER

What happens to human colonists crashed on a forbidden world when its brutal alien owners return?

The Taveshi see humans as an invasive species, and are debating exterminating us. Guess who they chose to represent humanity? Not a diplomat, a scientist, or even a politician. Just me, Tiffany Ranger, an eco-engineer with a smart mouth that keeps getting me into more trouble than I can handle.

I'd complain more if their captain, Skymaster Korovan, wasn't so damn irresistible. Seven feet tall, carefully carved muscles in all the right places. I know I shouldn't stare but, honestly, can you blame me? To make matters all the more difficult, he won't stop staring at me, either!

He's claimed me as his mate, but I'm no one's property. Though if I had to belong to someone, he'd be at the top of my list, especially if it would spare the rest of the humans on Crashland. Would it be so wrong to pretend, just for a little while? After all, it's just acting, and it's for a good cause. It's not like I'm going to get feelings for him…right?

JUDGED BY THE ALIEN SKYWARDEN

He's arrogant, aggressive and abrasive – and hotter than the surface of the Sun.

Which is a problem when I'm in a race against time in a test *he* set. If my team and I don't solve the puzzles scattered around Crashland by the deadline, our alien overlords will annihilate every human on the planet. I need to focus on that, not on the judge's amazing alien abs or what I want him to do with his tongue!

But Skywarden Darakar is huge, muscled all over, and dangerously attractive. I can't keep my eyes off him when we're together, or my mind off him when we're apart. The only consolation I have is that he's just as distracted by me.

And now someone is sabotaging the test. Darakar wants our trial to be fair, and I want to survive, so for now we're on the same side. But the more time we spend in each other's company, the harder it is to keep our hands off each other.

Judged by the Alien Skywarden *is book two of the Crashland Contact Romances. Each book is a complete story with no cheating and no cliffhangers – just steamy, exciting SciFi Romance.*

CLAIMED BY THE ALIEN SKYLORD

He's the enemy. He's irresistible. And I'm screwed.

I'm supposed to spy on him, but it's hard to look for his secrets when I can't keep my eyes off his abs.

Jadrok is heir to the mighty House Vragos, the alien nobles who own Crashland. Dark, brooding, and as hot as molten steel, he's a mystery calling out for me to unwrap. Unfortunately, my mission is more important than my need to touch his golden skin or taste his kisses.

It's my job to find out who's at the heart of the alien conspiracy to wipe out all the humans of Crashland. I can't afford to get distracted by an alien lord, especially when he might be one of the plotters.

No matter how attractive he is.

No matter how much he wants *me*.

Claimed by the Alien Skylord is book three of the Crashland Contact Romances. Each book is a complete story with no cheating and no cliffhangers – just steamy, exciting SciFi Romance.

SCI FI ROMANCE BY LESLIE CHASE

STANDALONE BOOKS

STRANDED HEARTS

There he is, bane of my life and wrecker of my sanity. The hottest alien in the galaxy, and the most punchable.

Prince Draxus of Tagra is the *worst*. Huge, charismatic, rich, and he's decided I'm his good luck charm. Only one problem – I'm supposed to be his bodyguard, not that he thinks he needs one.

Now we're stranded in a deadly crystal jungle, dressed for an interstellar cruise, and pursued by vicious pirates. It's my job to stay close to him, and that's given him the idea that I'm interested. Which I'm not! Certainly, definitely *not*.

… am I?

Oh no.

And worst of all, there's only one tent.

__Stranded Hearts__ is a scorching sci-fi romance novella featuring a badass heroine and a rugged alien prince who will do anything to protect her.

This story was initially published in the __Claimed Among the Stars__ anthology.

Written in the Stars

He might be the hottest guy in the galaxy, but I don't need his help. Me and my alien cat are managing just fine.

Running a bookshop on a pirate space station isn't easy, but Megan's determined to keep smiling. A lot of hard work and a bit of luck will let her save up enough for a trip back to Earth—but then Drask walks into her shop. The grumpy alien mercenary is infuriating, arrogant, and hotter than molten steel. It wouldn't be so bad if he wore more clothes—the blue-skinned alien's muscles are a distraction Megan doesn't need.

Talbrek Station is the perfect place to lie low, and that's what Drask needs after a mission gone wrong. Finding a bookshop is an unexpected benefit, especially one run by the sexiest woman he's ever seen. Exasperating, smart, and unwilling to back down from anything, Megan is everything Drask desires, wrapped up in a curvy package that won't let him think straight.

When the local criminals threaten both Megan's bookstore and her pet, Drask can't stand aside. Not even if it drags them both into a gang war.

__Written in the Stars__ was first published in the __Pets in Space__ 7 anthology, though this version has minor changes. It's a fast-paced science fiction romance story about finding love in unlikely places, with no cheating, no cliffhanger, and a happy ever after to make you smile.

OUTLAW PLANET MATES

Reazus Prime is a hard planet. Once a prison, it was abandoned once the mines dried up and the Overlords could no longer turn a profit off the prisoners. Now it's a haven for outlaws, pirates, and anyone holding a grudge against authority.

It's isolated, alone, and the only ships coming are the worst sort. One such ship carrying a cargo of abducted human women, explodes in orbit. A lucky few were ejected in pods, only to crash on the outlaw planet.

Now the race is on to find and claim the human females.

This shared-world series brings together a group of your favorite SFR authors, each writing their own stories in the same setting. Check out all the books on Amazon here:
Outlaw Planet Mates

ALIEN'S MERCY (OUTLAW PLANET MATES)

First, I was abducted by little green men, then abandoned on a prison planet, and finally captured by a band of alien slavers... and the day isn't even over! FML.

One of my alien captors is different, though. He's a man, yes, but he isn't green, and he's anything but little. Huge comes to mind. Breathtakingly big.

I shouldn't trust him.

I shouldn't lust for him.

And if he delivers on his promise to send me back to Earth, I don't know if I can bear losing him.

Alien's Mercy is a stand alone book in the Outlaw Planet Mates series. The books can be read in any order. No cliffhangers, no cheating and a HEA.

SILENT EMPIRE ROMANCES

Each of these books follows the story of a different woman, snatched from Earth and thrust into the Silent Empire — a galaxy-spanning nation of intrigue and romance. Read to see them find their alien mates amongst the stars.

Each of these books can be read as a standalone, though they share some characters.

Stolen for the Alien Prince, by Leslie Chase

Stolen from Earth, Hope must pretend to be the princess Xendar is expecting to mate with. But the alien warlord has hidden depths, and soon Hope isn't sure if she wants to escape after all!

Stolen by the Alien Raider, by Leslie Chase

Amy didn't believe in aliens until she was taken. Trapped on their spaceship, lightyears from Earth, her only ally is Kadran. He's there to bring down the ring of slavers, but once he sees the Earthwoman, she's all he cares about.

Stolen by the Alien Gladiator, by Leslie Chase

Abducted by aliens, sold at auction… can Emma's day get any worse? But one alien warrior, Athazar, will stop at nothing to protect her — even when they are forced into the arena to fight for their lives.

CELESTIAL MATES

Mated to the Alien Lord, a Celestial Mates novel by Leslie Chase

Love is never easy. Love on an alien world is downright dangerous!

With her life on Earth going nowhere, Gemma needs a fresh start. Enter the Celestial Mates Agency, who say they can match her with the perfect alien. And despite the dangers of his planet, Corvax is everything she could have asked for — impossibly hot, brave, and huge.

Now that she's seen him, there's no way she's going back.

Mated to the Alien Pirate

On the run from the mob – into the arms of an alien space pirate.

With alien mobsters hot on her trail, Marcie Cole needs a way off Earth fast. When the Celestial Mates Agency matches her with an alien on the far side of the galaxy, she jumps at the chance to get offworld. Her match may be a sexy alien, but she doesn't expect to like him. And she definitely didn't expect him to board her ship as the captain of a lethal crew of space pirates.

Pirate Captain Arrax is huge, deadly, and hot as hell. But can she trust a pirate to keep her safe, or should she hide the truth about herself?

DRAGONS OF MARS

by Leslie Chase & Juno Wells

The remains of the Dragon Empire have slumbered on Mars for a thousand years, but now the ancient shifters are awake, alive, and searching for their mates!

Each book can be read on its own, but you'll get the best effect if you read them in order.

1. **Dragon Prince's Mate**
2. **Dragon Pirate's Prize**
3. **Dragon Guardian's Match**
4. **Dragon Lord's Hope**
5. **Dragon Warrior's Heart**

WORLDWALKER BARBARIANS

by Leslie Chase & Juno Wells

Teleported from Earth to a far-off planet, found by blue skinned wolf-shifter aliens, and claimed as mates. Is this disaster or delight for the feisty human females?

1. **Zovak**
2. **Davor**

The Alien Explorer's Love, by Juno Wells & Leslie Chase

Can Two Beings from Different Worlds Find Common Ground — And Love?

Jaranak is an alien explorer on a rescue mission to Earth, but now he's stranded here at the dawn of the 20th century. And his efforts to go unnoticed are bring thwarted by Lilly, a human female who won't stop asking questions. She should be insufferable, but instead he finds himself unable to get the sassy woman out of his mind…

ABOUT LESLIE CHASE

LESLIE CHASE

I love writing, and especially enjoy writing sexy science fiction and paranormal romances. It lets my imagination run free and my ideas come to life! When I'm not writing, I'm busy thinking about what to write next or researching it – yes, damn it, looking at castles and swords and spaceships counts as research.

If you enjoy my books, please let me know with a review. Reviews are really important and I appreciate every one. If you'd like to be kept up to date on my new releases, you can sign up for my email newsletter on my website — subscribers get a free science fiction romance novella!

www.leslie-chase.com

- facebook.com/lesliechaseauthor
- x.com/lchasewrites
- bookbub.com/authors/leslie-chase
- goodreads.com/Leslie_Chase
- amazon.com/Leslie-Chase/e/B019S4QW3C

Made in the USA
Columbia, SC
13 May 2025